The United States Marshals Service

Formed in 1789 by President George Washington, the United States Marshals Service is the oldest federal law enforcement agency—and in my mind, one of the most mysterious. They used to carry out death sentences, catch counterfeiters—even take the national census. According to their Web site, "At virtually every significant point over the years where Constitutional principles or the force of law have been challenged, the marshals were there—and they prevailed." Now the agency primarily focuses on fugitive investigation, prisoner/alien transportation, prisoner management, court security and witness security.

No big mystery there, you say? When I started this series, I didn't think so, either. Intending to nail the details, I marched down to my local marshals' office for an afternoon that will stay with me forever.

After learning the agency's history and being briefed on day-to-day operations, I was taken on a tour. I saw an impressive courtroom and a prisoner holding cell. Then we went to the garage to see vehicles and bulletproof vests and guns. Sure, I'm an author, but I'm primarily a mom and wife. I bake cookies and find hubby's always-lost belt. Nothing made the U.S. Marshals Service spring to life for me more than seeing those weapons. And then I realized my tour guide wasn't fictional. He uses these guns, puts his very life on the line protecting me and my family and the rest of this city, county and state. I had chills.

Things really got interesting when I started digging for information on the Witness Security Program. Deputy Marshal Rick ever so politely sidestepped my every question. I found out nothing! Not where the base of operations is located, not which marshals are assigned to the program, what size crews are used, how their shifts are rotated—nothing! After a while it got to be a game. One it was obvious I'd lose!

Honestly, all this mystery prob[ably makes for better fiction. I] don't want to know what real[ly happens. It's not nearly as] romantic as the images of the[marshals I've dreamed up in my] mind. Oh, and another bonus[to my research—my tour guide] was Harlequin American Rom[ance...]

Laura Altom

Dear Reader,

This book was especially fun to write, as it's all about crushes. Charity's angst over whether or not Adam likes her as more than just a friend brought back fun—sometimes painful—memories of the crushes I've had.

My first crush was tall, blond Michael. For months I chatted and flirted with him, and when Valentine's Day came, I was super excited about the prospect of him maybe buying me one of the student council's fund-raising carnations. And can you believe it—it snowed and school was closed!

I was at my best friend Kristen's, shoveling her driveway, lamenting about how I'd never know if Michael liked me, when he and his dad pulled up in a car. Instead of one of the student council's stinky old carnations, I got a pretty crystal vase with three roses. How sad is it I don't remember what color? Anyway, a few days later, when Michael asked me to Go With Him (going-steady lingo then) I thought I'd died and gone to heaven. Charity feels the same way with Adam. Sadly, like my torrid, ninth-grade affair, Charity's contented glow lessens when she finally takes off her rose-colored glasses.

I didn't end up marrying my first big crush. As for Charity ending up with Adam...you'll have to read the book and see!

Laura Marie Altom

P.S. You can reach me through my Web site at www.lauramariealtom.com or write to me at P.O. Box 2074, Tulsa, OK 74101.

TO CATCH A HUSBAND

Laura Marie Altom

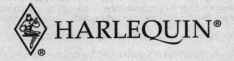

HARLEQUIN®

TORONTO • NEW YORK • LONDON
AMSTERDAM • PARIS • SYDNEY • HAMBURG
STOCKHOLM • ATHENS • TOKYO • MILAN • MADRID
PRAGUE • WARSAW • BUDAPEST • AUCKLAND

ISBN-13: 978-0-373-75127-3
ISBN-10:   0-373-75127-3

TO CATCH A HUSBAND

www.eHarlequin.com

Printed in U.S.A.

For United States Marshal Timothy D. Welch and
Deputy U.S. Marshal Rick Holden. Thank you for the
incredible tour of Tulsa's marshals' office, and for
patiently answering my gazillion questions.
Any technical errors are all mine.

And for Twon Beeson—even though you didn't
directly share your bubble gum story with me,
I still enjoyed it very much.

And for the ladies of Girls' Weekend 2005!
Lynne, Abbey, Holly, Denise, Sandy, Pam,
Katherine, Michelle, Diane—thanks for including
me in your crazy-fun tradition! You all rock!!

Books by Laura Marie Altom

HARLEQUIN AMERICAN ROMANCE

940—BLIND LUCK BRIDE
976—INHERITED: ONE BABY!
1028—BABIES AND BADGES
1043—SANTA BABY
1074—TEMPORARY DAD
1086—SAVING JOE*
1099—MARRYING THE MARSHAL*
1110—HIS BABY BONUS*

*U.S. Marshals

Chapter One

"No," Deputy U.S. Marshal Adam Logue said to the company shrink, sitting across from her in her second-story loft located in the center of Portland's artsy Pearl District.

"Now what kind of attitude is that?" The middle-aged woman eyed him with a concerned frown before consulting her clipboard. The clipboard on which she'd somsehow managed to cram everything that'd been going on in his head. Private stuff. Stuff he'd never told another soul—so how had it ended up there?

"Mr. Logue," Dr. Margaret Davey said, resuming her former all-business smile. "Or, Adam, if I may call you that?"

"Mr. Logue works for me."

"All right." She made a note on her clipboard.

Great. After that San Francisco shooting, all he needed was another mark on his record.

"Look," he said. "If I get brownie points for allowing you to call me by my first name, that's cool. I just—"

She wrote faster and faster.

"Did you hear me?"

She stopped. Looked up. "Sure, I heard you, Mr. Logue. My question for you is, are you hearing yourself? Because I'm sensing an enormous reserve of pent-up anger. But even more importantly—fear. Care to expand on that?"

"Well…" He leaned forward, gracing her with an acid smile. "I could tell you everything that led me here, but what's the point? You've got it all there on my chart."

"True, but I have someone else's version. What I'm after is your own."

"My version?" With a sharp laugh, he began. "Here goes. I fell for the wrong girl. She was shot and killed. I couldn't do a damn thing to save her. When I saw a guy threatening to whack my brother and the woman he loves, I shot him. I was doing my job as a U.S. Marshal. Am I angry? Hell, yeah. But not at the world. Not at the system. I'm mad at myself. I'm especially pissed my dad's behind this." He gestured to the sparse surroundings—the gray walls, the black-leather furniture. Even the curtains were gray, blocking out a gray Portland, Oregon, day. "Even though my old man's retired, he still plays golf with my boss. Over an afternoon of too much sun and beer, the two of them hatched this plan for me to get my head straight. So when you so cavalierly suggested I start dating again, my answer was no. Will always be—no."

"So then there's really no point in being here?"

"Right. Glad you finally see this my way." He pushed himself up from the stupid, too-soft black armchair he'd spent the past thirty minutes drowning in. "I take it the boss gets the bill?"

She nodded.

"Great. Have a nice life, and sorry if I come across as rough around the edges, but I'm not a touchy-feely guy. Never have been, never will be."

"Sit down, Mr. Logue. You're on my time, and I still have another thirty minutes."

He ignored her, heading for the door.

"Your boss feels that, because of what happened in San Francisco and years earlier with Angela Jacobs, you've become a shell of a person. A robot. Which, in turn, has affected virtually every area of your life—including your work. Would you say this is a fair assessment?"

"I'd say," he said, fingers clenched around the cold, brass doorknob, "it's none of your business—or Franks'. I do my job. Was cleared of any wrongdoing."

"Fair enough." Scribble, scribble. "More ortho-dox psychiatrists prefer slow, methodical treatment, but I've never been that long-suffering. Hence your prescription."

"My prescription?"

"Yes, earlier, when I suggested you resume dating, it wasn't just an idea I tossed out. I believe when a patient has fallen off their horse, they should climb right back—"

He marched across the room, planting his hands on her chair's armrests. "Angela isn't a freakin' horse. She's a flesh-and-blood woman who—"

"Are you even aware you're speaking of her in present tense? As if she's still alive?"

At the shrink's venomous words, Adam abruptly released her chair. Took about ten steps back, parking himself in the relatively safe back end of her office.

"Before next week," she said, "I'll expect you to have gone on one date. It doesn't have to be long or elaborate. Meeting a woman for coffee will do. But, Adam, whether you believe it or not, your boss is serious about getting you help. And after meeting with you today, I must say that in my professional opinion, his concerns are valid. Now…" She cleared her throat. "I believe I've sufficiently explained your assignment. Do you have any questions?"

Oh—he had questions. Such as, was this invasion of his personal life even legal? And how long would he be put in the slammer for kidnapping his boss, then forcing him to sit through an hour of this asinine psychobabble?

"All right, then." She stood and flashed him what he took as a pitying smile. "If you have no questions, I'll look forward to seeing you next week."

Not if he had anything to say about it.

"BUG," Adam complained, "you wouldn't believe the crap she said to me. I mean, it was as if I wasn't even in the room. I swear, the woman's got it in for me."

Deputy U.S. Marshal Charity Caldwell—"Bug," as friends, co-workers and family called her because of her vast insect collection—didn't look up from pinning the *Goliathus cassicus* she'd ordered off the Web. Wow, was he a beauty—the West African beetle, not Adam.

Well, Adam was a beauty, too. But not because of his gold iridescent wings. She snort-laughed.

"I'm pouring out my heart, here. What's so funny?"

"You had to be there," she said, attention back on her acquisition. Adam had been on this tirade for a good thirty minutes. And truthfully, though she felt for the guy, she'd heard enough. She agreed that he shouldn't be dating—at least no one but her. Charity loved him. Had loved him ever since their first stakeout when her foot-long chili dog fell out the van window—long story—and he'd given her his.

"Where have you been lately that I haven't?"

"Nowhere," she said. "'You had to be there' is a figure of speech."

"I knew it. While I was stuck in traffic getting to and from the shrink's, not to mention the time I wasted there, something good went down and I missed it. Let's hear it."

She rolled her eyes. Shoved her obnoxiously thick glasses higher on her nose.

"Tell me…" Like some powerful, long-legged cat, he sprung from his chair, lunging at her mounting plate. "Talk, or the cockroach gets it."

"It's not a cockroach, and—" *You're seriously invading my personal space.* For just a second she squeezed her eyes shut, breathing him in. Had any man in the history of manhood ever smelled this good? Adam's scent was this crazy-hot mixture of everything she loved. Being outside on cold rainy days, gun powder and fast-food hamburgers. In short, he was her total package—only to him, she was just another of the guys.

Why, oh, why, couldn't she love someone else? Why was Adam's eternally messy dark hair such a turn-on? Why did she melt with just one look into his chocolate-brown eyes? Why did his big old toothy grin turn her stomach upside down? And the biggest question of all—why did she love him when she wasn't even sure he realized she was a woman?

Okay, and maybe that wasn't the biggest question, because an even more burning question was, when her biological clock was tick, tick, ticking to the point she no longer had the luxury of being choosy, why couldn't she for once banish the guy from her heart?

"Spill," he continued to tease, taking the mounting plate from her lap, setting it on the coffee table.

"Adam…"

"Don't think I won't tickle you, because you know I will."

Before she had time to fight him, he'd wrestled her up and out of her chair, down to the floor, tickling her ribs and underarms until she couldn't breathe from laughing.

"Stop!" she shrieked. "I'll tell you!"

"'Bout time," he said, breathing heavy, straddling her hips. Crossing his arms with a look of utter victory, she wiped the smirk off his face by pulling her best wrestling move, flipping him off of her and square into the recliner.

"Ouch!" he complained. "What'd you do that for?"

"You told me to *spill*," she said with a sweet smile. "You just never said what."

"Anyone ever told you you're mean?"

"Been hearing it ever since I gassed my first water bug."

"That is pretty harsh," he said, leaning back against the recliner.

"My perfect sister thought so, too." But for as long as she could remember, Charity hadn't had a problem with any aspects of her predominantly male-oriented world—even if it meant gassing her own insect specimens. It wasn't something she liked thinking about, but she used to be a girly girl, hanging out with her mom and big sister while her twin brother, Craig, was tight with their dad. Then Craig had died when they'd been only seven. He'd fallen out of a tree house he and their dad had built that past summer.

It had taken her father a year and another summer to recover from Craig's death, and Charity liked to think that in large part, she'd been the reason Dad had begun to live again. Trouble was, in her heart of hearts, she knew that to her father she'd stopped being a daughter and had assumed the role of surrogate son. She'd taken up softball, stamp and bug collecting. Even as an adult, she still very much enjoyed her bugs—the hobby her father launched. The activity was calming. The camaraderie of sharing exciting new acquisitions with her dad—even if it was now mostly over the phone or Internet, seeing how he and her mom lived in Wyoming. The best part of the pastime was the order it brought to her world, where chaos typically reigned—at least where Adam was concerned.

Charity's dad was her hometown's sheriff, and he'd encouraged her to follow in his footsteps. And because she loved him—never again wanted to see hollow loss in his eyes—she'd done just that and made him proud. Sometimes, she feared, at the expense of her own dreams.

Don't get her wrong, she loved her work. Her work meant the world to her. It's just that lately she'd started wanting more. Which was where her whole baby craving came in.

The more she'd hung out with her dad and other guys, the easier it'd become. For most of her life, she felt more at home with guys than girls. Most guys, that is. Until meeting Adam. Adam bore the distinction of being the one man who made her crave being a woman. Therein lay the rub, seeing as how he thought of her as just another guy.

"Yeah," he said. "That lady doc today? She reminded me of your sis. Lots of makeup and hair that looked like it wouldn't budge in a stiff breeze. Could've been a fiftysomething hottie if she'd taken the know-it-all stick out of her butt."

Charity winced. Would Adam talk like that around a *real* girl? Not that she wasn't a real girl with all the requisite parts and needs, but—

"You want me to call in a pizza?"

"I thought the poor lady doctor with the stick in an unmentionable spot gave you an assignment?"

He shrugged, then reached for the cordless phone she'd left on an end table. He pressed the talk button. "Oh, man. It's dead. Bug, how many times do I have to tell you to put the phone back on the charger?"

"Sorry. Use your cell. Better yet, call from your own apartment."

"You know I like it more here. Besides, I'm under stress. You have to help me."

He was under stress? Ha! He didn't know the meaning. Staring out her fourth-floor condo's window at a steady autumn rain, she massaged her left hand with her right.

"Okay?" Adam asked.

She glanced his way, wishing she still didn't feel breathless from having him all over her. What would it feel like to have him on top of her for a purpose other than tickling? "Uh-huh," she said in response to his question. "Lately, the rain seems to make me stiff. Must be getting old, huh?" She grinned, but the statement held a sad truth. No, she wasn't ancient, but at thirty-five, if she wanted more from her life—husband, kids, house—it was time to get on with it.

From the same table where he'd found the dead phone, he grabbed a tube of pear-scented lotion her sister, Stephanie, had given her for her birthday. The only reason Charity had even opened it was because she'd run out of her usual generic brand.

He flipped open the green tube's top, waved it under his nose. "Nice." Glancing at the label, he whistled. "Victoria's Secret. La-di-da."

From her spot on the floor a few feet from him, Charity lunged for the lotion, but missed when he held it over her head. "Do you always have to be such a spaz?" she asked.

He flashed her one of his slow grins that were so breathtakingly gorgeous. They were really starting to tick her off. "As a matter of fact," he said, squeezing a dollop of lotion into his palm. "Yes, I do have to be a spaz. Which is precisely why you love me, right?"

Why did he do this? Spout words that to him meant nothing but to her—

She lost all capacity to think when he took her hands in his. He'd rubbed his hands together first, warming the amazing-smelling lotion, then smoothing it into her skin, methodically massaging each finger until she was nearly purring from pleasure.

"How's that feel?" he asked.

"G-good."

"You okay?" he asked.

"Sure. Why?"

"I dunno. You seem tense."

How would he feel if the tables were turned? If he'd loved her for as long as he could remember, then some buttinski shrink told her to start dating other men? But that was the problem. They weren't dating, and Adam didn't love her. So, yes. She was tense. Crazy tense. Which led her to say, "That's good. On my hands, I mean. You can stop."

"Sure?"

She nodded.

He released her, and once again she could breathe.

"I left my cell in the truck, so let me run out and get that and I'll call in an order. What do you want? The usual?"

"I guess." Look at them. They were like an old married couple—without the sex. Only, if Adam were hers, she'd want to—well, you know—every night of the week!

"You're grinning again," he said, pulling on a leather jacket before heading out the door. "When I get back, you'd better tell me what happened today, or else."

If by "or else," he meant he'd tickle her again? Charity would gladly take her chances.

SATURDAY NIGHT, Frederika, a Puerto Rican swimsuit model Adam met Friday afternoon while she was doing a promo thing at his favorite sporting goods store, glowered across the table at him. "Are you on purposefully trying to ruin our evening?"

"Um, no," he said, putting down his menu. It'd been two days since his shrink-mandated order to find himself a date. He'd done just that, and look, on his very first try, not thirty minutes into the evening, already it was a disaster. "Why?"

"First," she said, slapping down her menu, as well. "You show up dressed like…" With exaggerated Latin flair, she waved her hands. "A hobo—"

"A hobo?" He glanced down at his jeans and T-shirt. "This is one of my best tees. I even ironed it." Sort of. Seeing how he'd yanked it out of the dryer while it'd still been warm.

"And this place…" she said with a roll of her tongue, eyeing Ziggy's red walls lined with sports memorabilia and the light fixtures that'd been rigged from basketball halves. She probably wasn't much into the all-sports radio blaring, either. "Could you no have afforded better? And now, you tell me we must have beer with dinner, not wine? And your car was…how you say? Fill-thee." Her speech's grand finale was a theatrical shudder.

"Sorry," he said, nose back in his menu. Cheeseburger or ribs? Tough call.

"You should be sorry. Do you know how lucky you are to be with me? I could get another man just like that." She snapped her fingers. "I deserve better. You show me good time or I'll call my brother Rico. He tell you how to treat a woman."

Adam inwardly groaned.

"Well?" his date said, lifting razor-thin eyebrows. "You ready to take me to a nice place?"

Where Adam wanted to take her was straight back to her apartment, but a vision of his glowering shrink made him try to please.

"ADAM?" Charity opened her door as wide as the security chain would allow. "What're you doing here? It's the middle of the night."

"Only for homebodies like you," he said. "For normal people it's 8:00 p.m. So? You going to let me in?"

She closed the door to unfasten the chain, then opened it again, wishing she'd had the foresight to put on real clothes.

Once he'd helped himself to her sofa, then flicked on the end table lamp, he asked, "What're you wearing?"

"It's a nightgown."

"No," he said with a wink. "If I didn't know better, I'd say it was negligee. Your sis give you that to go with the Victoria's Secret lotion?"

"Yeah, what of it? I wouldn't even be wearing it if all my sweats weren't in the laundry."

"I'm not complaining," he said. "Looks good on you. You should wear it again sometime."

"F-for you?"

"Like friends with privileges?" He winked. "Hell, yeah!" A jab to her ribs showed her he was just joshing. So why wouldn't her pulse slow down? "Hey, you wanna order pizza? I'm starving."

She dropped onto the far end of the sofa, pulling her knees up to her chest, then wrapping her arms around bare legs, wishing the ivory satin-and-lace baby-doll-styled number had a couple more yards of fabric. "Thought you had a swanky dinner date tonight with that swimsuit model?"

"I did. But she didn't like Ziggy's Burger Barn, so I ended up having to take her to Swenson's—and you know how pricey that place is. I shelled out fifty bucks a head for an ounce of beef and a few mystery green squiggly things. Oh, and there was some freaky mushroom pile, drowning in gravy and carrot sprinkles. But she didn't like that, either. I was going to stop back by Ziggy's after taking Freddy home, but after all that mind-numbing talk about her hair, clothes and nails, I found myself craving pizza—and you."

"Flattery like that will get you everywhere," she

teased, plucking ten or so insect catalogs from the sofa so he could park himself beside her. "Well? You going to order?"

"Sure. The usual?"

"You know it."

He snatched the cordless phone from the coffee table, placed an order for a large pan pizza with the works, gave his credit card number, then hung up. Wandering into the kitchen, he grabbed a bag of potato chips from her snack cabinet. For an average person, this might've seemed odd, but Adam ate more than anyone on earth, so chips after a swanky dinner and before pizza was pretty much his norm. After popping two Hostess cupcakes, as well, he said, "And, hey, while we're waiting for the grub, I've got something I'd like to run by you."

"Shoot," she said, returning to the stag beetle she'd been pinning before Adam's interruption.

"Here's the deal…" He sat beside her, then reached for her hands. As focused as she'd just been on pinning her new acquisition, the shock of him again taking her hand so intimately jolted her to a whole 'nother place—the fantasyland she'd spun of the two of them. Her first instinct was to yank herself free, but instead she froze, like the last time he'd pulled this stunt, self-ishly indulging in the decadence of being held. "In the middle of this date with a strange, high-maintenance woman I knew after being alone with her for five minutes I never wanted to see again, I had a great idea."

"What's that?"

"Glad you asked," he said with a grin so potent, it took Charity a second to find her next breath. "The company shrink told me I had to date, right?"

"Yeah." He was still massaging her hands, flooding her with tingling pleasure.

"Well, the doc didn't say a thing about *who* I had to date—just that I had to go out with someone."

"And?" Charity said, blaming trace formaldehyde fumes for the dizzying heat.

"And—you're going to love this—so I figure, why don't I just go out with you?"

Chapter Two

Charity hadn't yet recovered from Adam's first ludicrous statement, when he kept going. "The beauty of this plan," he said, "is that not only do I get the doc off my back, but you're not going to expect anything of me, right? We can hang here. Or have nice, cheap dinners at Ziggy's. The way I see it, it's a win/win for both of us, seeing as you'll get free grub."

Charity snatched back her hands.

"No," she said, pushing herself up from the sofa. "I'm too busy."

In front of the now-dark view of Mount Hood that'd been the reason she'd forked over too much for this condo, she crossed her arms and tried hard not to give in to the knot swelling at the back of her throat.

"Too busy?" Adam laughed, leaving the sofa to join her. "What do you do besides hang out with me?"

"That's the point," she said, good and mad not only at his presumptuousness, but at herself for letting their relationship—or lack thereof—get to this level. She was tired of being his buddy. His pal. Dammit, she wanted to at least be his girl. And if she were totally honest with herself, in her wildest dreams, what she really wanted was to someday be his wife. Have his babies. "Is it so wrong of me to want more?"

"More?" He coughed. "What's that mean?"

"Want me to spell it out?"

"Might be nice."

"Okay. First off, do you have any idea how long it's been since I've been on a date?"

"No."

"Well, I'll tell you. Over three years. And that's just sad. Night after night, I sit here, listening to all your problems, Adam, and never once do I saddle you with mine."

"You could," he said, grinning, landing a friendly slug to her upper arm. "You know I'd be here for you—anytime. Come on, give me a few. I'm all ears."

"All right, for starters, I'm around men all the time, yet they don't see me as a woman, but just another guy. I know I've got to do something to change that perception, but just the thought is overwhelming."

"Huh?" Sitting again, he leaned against the sofa back. "Are you PMSing? You're acting a little mental."

"Thanks," she said. She was really on a roll. "That helps a lot. Okay, next problem—since you mentioned PMS—I just had a physical, and my doctor asked if I plan on starting a family. Next, she launches into this speech on how if kids are something I want in my future, I might want to get on with it. She then proceeded to point out just how drastically the odds of fun stuff like birth defects increase the older women get. Geesh, I'm only thirty-five, so I ask, aren't women having babies at fifty? But then—"

"Whoa," Adam said, making a T with his hands. "Time out. You? Want babies? As in someone a foot tall calling you 'Mommy'?"

"Is that so hard to believe?"

He sobered. "Not at all, it's just… Well, I never thought of you in that way."

"What *way?*"

"You know…nurturing. Tucking little humanoid beings in for the night. Making sure they take their vitamins in the morning, helping with homework. When are you going to have time for you? And work? Let alone me?"

"Adam?" The laugh crinkles at the corners of his eyes had her smacking him over the head with her ladybug throw pillow. "You're such a jerk."

"Sorry," he said. "But you've always been one of the guys. It never even occurred to me you'd go the family route."

"Family *route?* You think a dream I cherish is some stupid route?"

"I never said that—and I sure as hell never said it was stupid. You'd make a great mom. But, babe, how do you expect guys to think of you as anything other than a guy when all you ever do is guy stuff? Play video games and watch ESPN. Slave over your bugs. I mean, if you want some dude to like you—in a baby-making way—maybe you should put on a dress. You know, let him know you're interested. Speaking of which, got anyone special in mind for the daddy?"

Someone knocked on the door. The pizza guy?

"That was fast," Adam said, relief in his voice at the interruption. As long as Charity had known him, he'd never been all that keen on sharing emotions. Lucky her, it looked as if he wasn't about to change tonight. "To show how sorry I am about the baby crack, I won't even ask you to pay half the bill."

"Maybe it'd be best if you just left."

"What do you mean?" he asked, expression dumbfounded. "The pizza just got here."

"Just go," Charity said, arms crossed, having a devil of a time trying not to cry as the realization of what she'd just done hit her. Blurting out she wanted a baby like that. Nuts. That's what that was. "I seriously want you to leave."

"But—"

"Please," she said. *Before I not only spill my deepest, darkest secret about loving you, but start blubbering, too.* "Go."

Adam stood, pizza in hand, in front of the open door. "Sure that's what you want?"

Swallowing hard, Charity nodded.

For the longest time he just stood there in the chilly hall, staring. The cool air raised goose bumps on her miles of bare skin, but she didn't care. Why, she couldn't say, but something about her asking him to leave had been akin to drawing her own personal line in the sand.

She'd only just now realized it, but enough was enough. She couldn't go on this way anymore. Doing the same old things. Following the same old routines. If she was ever going to make more of her life—stop being the son her father wanted and discover the woman she knew herself deep in her soul to be—now was the time.

With his free hand, using just tip of his index finger, Adam stroked heat from her shoulder to elbow, causing her to shiver both inside and out. "I'm worried about you. But if it's space you want, you got it."

Dying a thousand tiny deaths over his unexpected kindness, she almost called him back inside. Almost. But what would that have served other than to prolong her pain? They'd never be a couple—not the way she wanted. The sooner she got that fact through her head, the better off she'd be.

He wagged the pizza box, shot her a heart-stoppingly handsome grin, then headed down the long hall.

Closing the door, sliding the chain lock into place, lingering scents of Adam and sausage-and-mushroom pizza flavoring the air, Charity finally gave in to her tears.

SUNDAY AFTERNOON, Adam was drowning his sorrows in football and a bowl of chili—he'd wanted queso, but Bug wasn't answering her phone and he couldn't remember the recipe—when the doorbell rang.

Opening the door, he said, "Bug?"

"Sorry," his dad said with a chuckle, barging his way in with a bag overflowing with green stuff. "Better luck next time."

"Yeah, right." Adam muted the TV, then reclaimed his usual end of the sofa. His dad, a retired marshal, set his bag on the small table in what the official apartment complex guide called the dining nook, then lowered himself into the recliner. "What's up?"

"Just curious how your trip to the head doctor went. You were supposed to call."

"Guess I forgot."

"Well?"

"Want chili?" Adam asked, reaching to the coffee table for his empty bowl, taking it to the kitchen for a refill.

"No, thanks. I spent the morning at the Briar Street Farmer's Market with Cal and Victoria. You remember her? Allie's mom." Cal was his oldest brother Caleb's son—the son he hadn't met till the kid was eight! Allie was Caleb's wife. Caleb, also a marshal, had recently discovered he'd fathered a child when assigned to protect Allie, a judge. It blew Adam's mind to think the woman had kept Cal from his father all those years. Still, seeing how the two of them had

long since worked it out, Adam wasn't one to inter-
fere, or to dwell on the past.

Ha! His conscience had a field day with that one.

Other folks' pasts didn't plague him. His own,
however, was a burden he feared he might always bear.

Focusing on his old man rather than his own short-
comings, Adam raised his eyebrows. "Was this a date?"

"No, no." His dad looked away and coughed. "Just
a friendly outing with our grandson. That sack over
there's packed with veggies. Victoria says us men
need more antioxidants."

Adam grinned. Who knew the old guy still had it
in him to charm the ladies?

"It's your date I'm here about," his dad said.
"How'd Saturday night go? Caleb and Beau said this
Frederika was a real looker." Count on his nosy
brothers to be the ones spilling Adam's private life
to the one person he didn't want knowing about it.
His second oldest brother, Beau, was also a marshal,
and carried the Logue family trait of sticking his
nose where it didn't belong.

"Should be a looker," Adam said with a grunt.
"She's a swimsuit model." He turned the volume
back up on the game. Seahawks vs. Jets. Sadly, the
Jets were ahead by three touchdowns.

"And…you going out again?"

"Not that it's any of your business, but no. She's
pretty high maintenance. Not my type."

"What's Bug say?"

"Huh?"

"You know," his dad pressed. "About the date. Does she think you should ask Frederika out again?"

Adam turned up the TV.

AT WORK MONDAY, Charity did everything in her power to steer clear of Adam. Which was tough, seeing as how their team had just been assigned to a major drug case being tried in federal court. The defendant had been caught with more than thirty-two kilos of cocaine in his vehicle. As a statement to the jurors, the prosecution displayed the mounds of neatly packaged coke in the courtroom.

The boss wanted marshals on hand to dissuade anyone who'd calculated the drug's street value and thought it worth the risk to steal.

All day, Charity stood at the back of the courtroom, dressed in her baggy black suit that, okay, did probably come across as a trifle masculine. But geesh, was she supposed to have shown up to guard the goods in a miniskirt? Trying to avoid eye contact with Adam, who'd been posted behind the judge, had only added to the fun.

Talk about awkward.

"Yo, Bug." Her friend and fellow marshal, Bear, ducked into her office cubicle after court had been adjourned for the day and the defendant escorted "home" for the night. "We're headed to Ziggy's. Wanna go?"

"No, thanks," she said, not looking up from the report she'd been trying to finish for the past week.

"Your loss," Bear said. A few minutes later the giant sweetheart who shaved his head because he thought it made him look meaner, was back. "Seen Adam?"

She shook her head.

"If you do, tell him—"

"Okay," she snapped. "Do you mind? I'm trying to work."

"*Ex-cuuu-uuse* me," he said. "What bug crawled out of your collection and up your—"

"Cut her some slack," Adam said to Bear, barging into her cubicle, helping himself to the microwave popcorn she'd popped more to keep her mouth busy than because she'd been hungry.

"Tell her to cut *me* some slack," Bear said. "All I did was ask her to hang with us at Ziggy's and she bit my head off."

"She's sick, okay?" Adam said.

"What's wrong with her?"

"Um, guys? Hello?" Charity waved. "I'm sitting right here."

"Well?" Bear asked Charity. "What's wrong with you?"

"Nothing. Now, would both of you please leave, so I can get some work done."

"I thought you told me you had woman problems?" Adam said. "You know, all that stuff about how you want to get pregnant but—"

"What's wrong with you?" she asked Adam, shoving back her chair so hard she rammed it into the cubicle's back wall and, in the process, managed to knock down a few thick procedural guides. "I told you that in private. Why couldn't you keep your big mouth shut?" Standing, snatching the mini-backpack she used for a purse, she shot both men her dirtiest look, then headed for the door.

"She's pregnant?" Bear asked Adam once Bug was out of earshot.

"Nah," Adam said, finishing off her popcorn, wondering what he'd said to tick her off this time. "At least, I don't think so. Guess she could be, but who could be the dad?"

"I dunno," Bear said. "Only guy she ever hangs with is…" He looked straight at Adam and grinned. "Congratulations, man. I didn't even know you and Bug were an item. Well, I knew you two hung together, but—"

"Cut it out," Adam said, taking off after her.

Dammit, Bug was his best friend. What had happened between Sunday morning at her apartment and now? All he'd done was ask her to pretend to be his date. Had that really been so much to ask?

Hell, he'd helped her move—twice! Seemed to him that'd been a whole lot harder than a measly few nights out on the town.

He just couldn't deal with going on a string of meaningless dates. Casual, he could do. But putting himself out there in a romantic way hurt too damn much—especially because no matter how hard he tried, nearly a decade later, he just couldn't seem to work through what'd happened to Angela.

He'd met her while on assignment. Her dad was a high-powered judge, and death threats had been made against not just him, but his wife and only daughter. Adam, who was twenty-five at the time and easily blended in with her college crowd, had been assigned to be her closest contact.

Adam had always considered himself to be a man's man, not easily swayed by batting eyelashes or pouty lips. But one look at Angela and he'd been a goner. Even though he'd known getting involved with her was against the rules, when she'd showed classic signs of interest, he'd fallen hard. They'd managed to keep things under wraps for a while, but pretty soon, with Angela wired for sound, his boss caught on to the fact that every time her mike cut out, Adam had been cutting in. Lord, but they'd had some hot make-out sessions in her sorority house attic.

He'd tried, for Angela's safety—and his sanity—to cool things down, but that had only made her want to be with him all the more. God help him, he'd felt the same. He'd loved her. For the first time ever, he'd known what it was like to be willing to die for someone.

He'd been pulled off the case. Then, over a candlelit frozen lasagna dinner at his apartment, asked her to marry him. With an excited squeal, she'd accepted.

Adam had expected trouble from her family—he was far from her social standing—but to the contrary, her dad had been a self-made man, working two jobs to get through law school, and he'd adored Adam. He'd also loved the fact that Adam wasn't one of Angela's typical spoiled frat boys. Despite ever-increasing death threats, Angela's mother had launched plans for a wedding fit for royalty. She'd been warned it wasn't safe. But she'd said a life lived in fear wasn't worth living. Adam had admired the hell out of her moxie, yet he'd worried.

The size of the family's security detail doubled.

Still, Adam worried.

Worried to the point that Angela had moved in with him, because he believed with his entire being no one could keep her as safe as him. After all, no one else could have comprehended loving her as he had.

But in the end, the security hadn't been enough.

His love? That hadn't done squat.

On a blustery Tuesday afternoon, hustling to interview a wedding consultant, Angela had been shot outside Adam's apartment door. He'd been right beside her. Two other marshals had flanked her. Four other marshals had covered the stairwell and parking area. The coward-ass sniper had shot through them all. Hit Angela straight through her heart. She was supposed to have been wearing a vest, but had whined it made her look fat. Yeah, well, there in his arms, she'd looked dead. And there wasn't a damned thing—

Swallowing hard, willing himself to breathe, Adam squeezed his eyes shut.

He'd let her down. Yeah, she should've worn the vest, but he should've insisted. Made a game out of putting it on her himself.

Should've. Would've. Could've.

He could second-guess himself till the end of time, but the end result would still be the same. For all practical purposes, he'd killed the woman he'd loved. And now he would pay the consequences—for the rest of his freakin' life.

Sure, on the outside, he came across as a happy-go-lucky guy, but inside, he knew damned well he was damaged goods. Which was why it was so important for him to keep things right between him and Bug. He didn't deserve another chance at love, but surely even screw-ups like him deserved a best friend.

Which was exactly what Bug had become.

He caught up with her in the parking garage just as she was about to climb into her company-issued black SUV. "You're fast," he said.

"Why are you here?"

"My car's parked next to yours."

"And that's it?"

He sighed, wiped his face with his hands. "We're together every Sunday, right?"

"Usually. But what does that have to do with why you followed me?"

"I didn't follow you," he said. "I just pointed out I was parked next to you."

"Okay. Great. See you tomorrow." She opened her door and climbed in behind the wheel.

"Wait."

She sighed. "Adam, I'm really tired. It's been a long day."

"Yeah, I know. But yesterday, having to watch football without you—or your Velveeta dip—now *that* was a long day."

Lips pressed tight, she rolled her eyes.

"Seriously, with both my brothers married and most of the other guys I know either in a serious relationship or rooting for another team, Sunday afternoon I realized just how alone I really am. The game was a blow-out, so I turned off the TV and went for a long walk. Thought about a lot of stuff. About how maybe instead of constantly grieving Angela's death, I should celebrate her life. But what I can't figure is how I'm supposed to do that if I have to be out wasting my time with women I don't even like."

"Adam," Charity said. "I'm really tired. Where are you going with this?"

"Where am I going?" He laughed. "Bug, don't

you see? When I'm with you, losing Angela doesn't hurt half as much. But when I'm not with you, I feel…" He looked away. "I'm bad at this. *Really* bad."

"How do you feel, Adam? Tell me." *Please.* God knew she felt for Angela. Her too brief shining life. But were Adam to be granted the miracle of one more talk with her, Charity felt certain the woman would've told him to get on with things. To have a life. As he was, he just sort of wandered, not really living. Not really dying. Just being. If Angela had loved Adam even half as much as he'd loved her, she would never have wished this limbo on him. Worse yet, as much as Charity loved Adam, his limbo was now her own. "Tell me, Adam. How do you feel?"

"Okay…" He scratched his stubbled chin. "Raw. Guess that about sums it up. Is that how you are? You know, about all that baby stuff you brought up the other night?"

She didn't answer.

"Bug?"

"That's not my name."

"Sorry. *Charity.* Is that what's going on with you?" He stood in front of her, one hand holding the suit jacket he'd had to wear in court over his shoulder, the other tucked into the pocket of his dark slacks. He'd locked his beautiful brown gaze with hers, and though Charity wanted to look away, she couldn't. "Well?"

"Yeah," she said. "That's exactly how I feel—not that there's a lot I can do about it."

"Want me to fix you up with someone?"

She shook her head. "How about you? I heard one of the clerks in Judge Baker's office just got divorced."

"Nah. Too much baggage. What I was really hoping is we could just hang out. You know, so things go back to the way they were."

"How's that going to help either of us?"

"I don't know," he said, breaking his stare, with his free hand, thumping her open door's window. "Sorry I ever even brought it up."

So was she. Because no matter how insulted she was that he obviously didn't think of her as a woman, she couldn't get past the idiotic craving she had to go along with his plan. But why help scam his psychiatrist? How would that help Adam? And what about her? How would it feel to only pretend to be his date, knowing she didn't have a shot at being the real thing? Better yet, follow her original plan to remain just friends? Maybe even sever that tie in favor of finding someone else to declare her best friend? Like a woman who might actually understand some of what she was going through?

"Wanna go with the rest of the gang to Ziggy's?" he asked.

Yes. "Thanks," Charity said, "but I don't think so. Not tonight."

"Sure? It's all-you-can-eat baby back ribs night."

She loved ribs. Would it really hurt to pal around with Adam just one more night?

If she were truly serious about finding a husband instead of a guy friend—yes.

"HOW COME you're not with Adam?" her big sister, Stephanie, asked that night. She sat on the foot of her bed, painting her toenails Tequila Pink.

"Since when is tequila pink?" Charity asked, reading the name on the bottom of the bottle.

"Probably since the color designers ran out of legitimate pinks. Now, nice try at changing the subject, but you never, ever come to see me on a weeknight unless you need money. So out with it. How much are you short this month and what exotic bug am I helping to import?"

"There are no bugs and can't I come see you because I miss you?"

"Sure. I'd love it if that were the real reason you're here." She put the final coat on her last toe, then screwed the lid on the bottle. Holding it out to Charity, she asked, "Want to do yours?"

"No, thanks."

"Different color?" she asked, pointing Vanna White-style at her vast array of polish.

"Steph?"

"Yes?" Duck-walking so as not to muss her toes, she headed to her closet for a dress to wear on her date with Dr. Larry, a pediatrician. This was her first real relationship since her amicable divorce with her stockbroker ex, Todd. He was East Coast, she was West, and the two never really met halfway.

"This is going to sound strange," Charity said. "But do you think I'm pretty?"

"Of course."

"That was weak. Like you're just saying that because you're my big sister. Come on, I can take it. Tell me the truth."

"Sweetie…" Steph returned to the bed, put her hands on Charity's knees. "If you'd let me have my way with your clothes and hair and makeup for a couple hours, you wouldn't be just pretty, but gorgeous."

"Now I know you're just saying that to make me feel better."

"Wanna bet? And what brought all of this on? You've never given two figs about your appearance. I've always envied that in you. Your knack for being yourself."

"Yeah, well…" Charity made a face. "Right about now, being me sucks. All my mixed-up feelings are thanks to Adam." She told her sister what had transpired between her and her supposed best friend—stressing the part about how mortifying it'd been that here she's crazy in love with him, yet he only sees her as a pal who'd be handy for duping his shrink.

"And so you turned down his proposal?" Steph asked.

"He didn't propose! He asked me to be his fake date!"

"I know," her sister said. "You get what I mean. His proposal for the two of you to pretend date."

"Of course, I turned him down," Charity reasoned. "You think I shouldn't have?"

"Well…" In the bathroom, Steph expertly wielded her hair-straightening iron. "Seems to me, if you're serious about having a baby and husband, maybe you're going about this all wrong. What if you agreed to be Adam's date, only to show him how fantastic the two of you could be on another level?"

"Oh, please." Playing around with her sister's eyeliner, Charity said, "How am I going to do that when he doesn't even see me as a woman?"

"That's a cop-out," Steph said. "I'll guarantee if you doll yourself up, he'll see you differently. And another thing, you're scared that even if you make an effort to transform yourself into a bona fide hottie, Adam still won't get the message. And then what?"

"I'm not scared," Charity said. "Of anything." Except maybe missing her window of opportunity.

She wasn't sure why she wanted kids. Because as Adam had pointed out, raising them would take up a huge chunk of her time. Work would be logistically tough. But knowing that didn't stop the wanting. The yearning every time some lucky woman returned from maternity leave, brandishing her newborn, passing him or her around. When Charity took her turn and felt the trusting warmth against her chest, the impossibly soft scents of lotion and powder, and cute little clothes, she wanted a baby all her own, all the more. Along with the adoring husband proudly standing nearby, lugging around baby equipment.

That was the eternal problem. Sure, in this day and age, all Charity had to do to get a baby would be to pay a visit to the local sperm bank. Surely a town the size of Portland had one, or a dozen. But what was the fun in having a baby if she didn't have anyone to share it with? Meaning what she really wanted in her greedy heart of hearts was the total package. The perfect little family to match her already perfect job.

Charity pitched the eyeliner in the cosmetics basket and headed for the bathroom door. "I'd better get going and let you finish dressing for your big date."

"You don't have to leave," Steph said. "In fact, why don't you come with us? Larry's been saying he'd like to meet you."

"Thanks," Charity said at the door to her sister's bungalow. "But I've got a big night. Just got a *Eupatorus gracilicornis* in from Thailand that needs mounting."

"Okay, but if you ever want to take me up on that makeover, I'll be here. Seriously, Charity, enough's enough where Adam's concerned. Not that it's any of my business, but it's high time you gave the man a wake-up call."

That made Charity laugh.

"What's so funny?"

"The notion of Adam ever realizing we could be so much more than friends. In fact, I set him up with someone in the hopes of him moving on. That way, maybe I could move along, as well."

Steph rolled her eyes.

"WHO WAS THAT?" Bear asked Adam on Tuesday as they filed back into the courtroom after the noon recess.

"Oh, you mean the redhead I did lunch with?" Adam asked.

"Duh. She was hot. A scorcher."

Adam shrugged. "True. Bug hooked us up. But truthfully, while she's easy on the eyes, and from what I read between the lines, a closet nympho, I thought by the end of it, my ears were gonna bleed. Blah, blah, blah… If I'd had to hear one more thing about her demon ex, I'd have gnawed my hand off to get it out of her whiny clutches. What I wouldn't have given to just do lunch with Bug."

"What's up with you two?" Bear asked, holding open the door while Adam stepped through.

"Long story. Don't ask."

All through the afternoon session, Adam was forced to stare at Bug. His best friend. Who for some unknown reason since Sunday morning had pretty much refused to speak to him—except for setting up his lunch from hell. Which, come to think of it, she might've done it for spite.

He didn't get it. One minute they'd just been palling around, and the next, Bug acted as though he had the plague—at the very least a nasty flu.

Once court was out, he waited around the office until most everyone had left but her.

Enough was enough.

One way or another, he was going to get to the bottom of what was bugging his Bug.

"Hey," he said, holding out an unpopped bag of microwave popcorn. "Peace offering?"

"Thanks, but I'm not hungry."

"What are you, then?" He sat on the edge of her desk, playing with her collection of wind-up bug toys. He wound a jumping cricket, then let it go.

"What's that supposed to mean? And quit messing with my stuff before you—*aggghh!*"

Crash!

The already struggling ivy she'd kept alive for two years crashed to the floor. The terra-cotta pot was in twenty pieces, mixed in with dirt and crumpled leaves, and the still-jumping mechanical cricket topped the whole mess. Adam lay alongside it, having lunged to the floor to catch the pot, ultimately making things worse.

"Oops," he said, rubbing his aching lower back.

"Are you all right?" she asked, instantly out of her chair and on her knees beside him.

"I've been better. Sorry."

"It's okay," she said, "I'm just glad you're not

hurt. But you should be. I told you to quit messing with stuff."

"Wish you'd have been more forceful about it." Adam winced. "Well? Aren't you going to offer to kiss my ouchie?"

"You sure you didn't conk your head instead of your behind?"

The office's perfect Robocop of a marshal strolled up with a smirk on his face. "Figures it was you two causing the commotion," said the guy Adam secretly called Suck-up Sam.

"Move along," Adam said. "Show's over."

"Need help?" Sam said to Bug, holding out his hand to assist her over the debris heaped at her feet.

"I'm good," she said. "But thanks for asking."

"You bet." He winked at her. Winked!

Once Sam was out of earshot, Adam said, "God, that guy makes my teeth hurt. He's such a tool."

"I like him," she said. "He's always seemed nice."

Adam rolled his eyes. "Come on, I'll help clean up."

"You'll *help?*" Eyebrows raised, she said, "Correct me if I'm wrong, but aren't you the cause of this mess? Sam!" she called. "I need you, after all!"

Like a bad smell, Pretty Boy silently appeared, holding out his hand for Bug to take—which she did!

After he'd helped her step over the dirt and debris, he said, "I was just heading out for a bite to eat. Care to join me?"

"No, thanks," Adam said. "We're busy."

"Speak for yourself," Bug said, gazing up at the guy with the smile she usually only used when downing Ziggy's chocolate malts. "You broke it, you clean it."

Sam said, "See ya, Adam."

Bug didn't say anything, just waved.

Fury didn't begin to describe the emotion bubbling in Adam's gut. Then again, maybe it was lingering aftereffects of too much Sunday-afternoon chili? Either way, watching Suck-up Sam mosey off with his best friend didn't set well.

At all.

Now the only question was, what, if anything, was he going to do about it?

Chapter Three

A wolf whistle greeted Charity on her trek through the office Wednesday morning.

"Damn, Bug." Bear abandoned his coffee to chase after her. "What'd you do to yourself?"

"Why? Do I look that bad?" she asked, self-consciously trying to shove up her thick glasses, which were no longer there due to new contacts. Maybe taking such drastic steps with her appearance hadn't been such a hot idea? Easing into a new look might've been the best way to go.

"You look that *good,*" he said with a laugh. "Adam see you yet?"

"No? Why?" Just the mention of Adam's name sent her pulse racing. What if he didn't like her changes? The honey-blond, flirty flip cut that replaced her usual messy, mousy ponytail. The makeup her sister taught her to use that made her green eyes look huge. The emerald-green silk camisole and form-fitting black suit jacket and short skirt that would probably get her fired. Worst of all were the black heels she'd have to kick off should she have need to chase bad guys across the crowded courtroom.

Seeing Adam's reaction to Sam asking her for a date had been all the impetus she'd needed to take this last step in attempting to take their relationship to a new level. Granted, she was no expert, but even she'd seen Adam hadn't liked another man paying attention to her. Which had been her cue to once and for all make a play for him, or forever quit mooning and get on with her life.

Bear just chuckled, then went back to his coffee.

His reaction left Charity wishing for an earthquake—nothing major, just something big enough to open a hole large enough to swallow her.

"Looking good," Adam's brother, Beau, said on his way to the holding cell.

Adam's brother, Caleb, winked on his way to see the boss. "Hot stuff."

Oh, Charity felt hot all right! Hot enough to melt through the office floor without the help of a natural disaster!

"Stop," Sam said.

"W-why?" She froze. "Is there an escapee aiming a stolen gun at me?"

He laughed. "I want you to stop so I can look at you. You're stunning."

"Um, thanks," she said, cheeks blazing.

"You've always been pretty, but now…" He shook his head and grinned. "I'm blown away."

"Knock it off. I don't look that different."

"Yeah, Bug. You do." Adam stepped out of Caleb's office, file folder in hand, his expression stormy and unreadable.

Charity's breath caught in her throat. What did that face mean? Did he hate her new look? So what if he did? Why should she care? Every other guy in the office seemed to think she looked okay. Better than okay judging by Sam's reaction.

According to her sister's instructions, she was supposed to apologize to Adam first thing this morning, then offer to help with his dating dilemma. In retrospect, she wasn't so sure. It was as if something between them had irrevocably changed.

They used to be best friends. Able to talk about anything, but now…

"Say, Charity?" Sam asked. "There's a new Italian place that just opened down the street. Want to share an early supper after work?"

"Sure," she said, never breaking Adam's stare.

"Sounds great," Adam said to Sam, "but Bug's busy after work."

"Her name is *Charity*," Sam said. "And if she were busy, she wouldn't have accepted my invitation."

"Your invitation isn't worth—"

"Adam!" Charity said. "Stop it. What's wrong with you?"

Good question, Adam thought. "Nothing's wrong with *me*," he said, dragging her by her upper arm into Caleb's office, then shutting the door in Sam's gaping face. "But I can't begin to guess what's going on with you."

She sighed. Crossed her arms. "That was rude."

"Oh—" He laughed. "And it wasn't rude of old Suck-up out there to horn in on our standing Wednesday night…" What did they call their ritual Wednesday nights together? Ziggy's had all-you-can-eat boiled shrimp, and draft beers were only a quarter. The sticky-fingered, laugh-a-minute nights weren't dates, but sacred all the same.

"Our standing Wednesday night what, Adam? I told you I want to start a family. How am I going to do that hanging out at Ziggy's with you and Bear?"

Sam pounded on the door. "Logue, that move wasn't at all professional."

Adam rolled his eyes. "If he were a real man, he'd kick the door down and claim you."

"You know…" Shaking her head, Charity said, "I came in here today, ready to apologize. I'm sick of fighting with my best friend. I figured what the hey? Why not help with your dating problem? But seeing how you're behaving, why should I help when you're obviously not the slightest bit interested in helping me?"

Before Adam could stop her, or even come close to figuring out what she was upset about, she'd left him to join Sam, who'd been waiting for her out in the hall like a lost puppy.

Because he didn't know what else to do, Adam clenched his fists. Dammit. Why had he reacted like that over nothing more than Bug changing her hair-style and wearing a dress?

So what if she went out with Sam? It wasn't as if Adam had any claim on her. And if she was right, if he was her true friend, he'd wish her well in finding a guy who'd give her the family she all of a sudden wanted.

If he was her true friend, he'd apologize for going off on her like that. Then he'd do something grand as a follow-up. Really, spectacularly *huge*. Something big enough to prove he wasn't just saying sorry, but truly meant it. And not only that he was sorry about his latest explosion, but most especially back at her condo when he'd been less than enthusiastic about her confession about wanting kids. Which, looking back on it, had been the spark that'd ignited this whole feud. If a baby was what she wanted, then he was one-hundred percent behind her decision.

Even if that meant she'd end up with some guy like Sam?

Adam groaned.

Obviously he hadn't thought that far ahead, but for the moment anyway, he and Bug needed to at least get back on speaking terms. Then he'd broach the subject of her getting a kid via sperm bank or adoption!

AFTER COURT ADJOURNED for the day, Charity returned to her cubicle to see a dozen roses in a gorgeous crystal vase accompanied by a small white box.

Heart hammering, assuming the items were from Sam, but hoping, praying, they could be from Adam, who'd glowered at her across the crowded courtroom all through the excruciatingly long day.

First, she plucked the card from the roses, berating herself for trembling hands. Geesh, from the way she was reacting, you'd think she'd never gotten roses before—which she hadn't.

The card read:

> The heaviest insect is the African Goliath
> beetle, which can weigh as much as nearly
> a quarter of a pound. But then obviously
> whoever made that claim hasn't seen
> the newest bug in your collection.
> Sorry for being a dung beetle.
> I miss you. Your friend, Adam

Tears stung Charity's eyes.

The note was classic Adam. The flowers were not. How had he even figured out how to call a florist, let alone arrange for delivery? The gesture smacked of his sister, Gillian. Sticking with the Logue family job, she was still a part-time marshal, but also a wife and mom. And since marrying a great guy, Joe, she also happened to be loaded. Meaning, if ever there was an extravagant gift around, Gillian and Joe were usually the ones to thank.

Charity deeply inhaled the roses' rich scent before moving on to the box. Finding flowers was one thing, but finding a rare beetle she didn't already have was another. Had Adam found her an Indonesian *Euchirus longimanus?*

Lifting the lid, at first the only things she saw were mounds of pink tissue paper. Then she dug deeper to find keys and a picture of an adorable black VW convertible bug.

No way…

Heart hammering, she looked up, and there was Adam, standing at the opening to her cubicle, wearing his most heartstopping sexy-slow grin. "Don't suppose I could catch a ride home?"

"I-Is this for real?" she asked.

He shrugged. "Real as you want it to be. I've been a jackass, and in order to show you how sorry I am, I kinda felt something along this scale would be appropriate."

"B-but you can't afford to buy me a car on your salary, Adam."

"Yeah, well, I know a couple who give super loan rates. Gil and Joe were only too willing to help, seeing how much they've both always liked you. And they agree with me that when you do finally have a baby, you should have a reliable car."

"You told them? About how I want to—"

"They won't tell anyone else."

"That's not the point. You just can't go around—"

Before she could get out further objections, he kissed her. Fast. Hard. Deliciously, surprisingly thorough. "Just say thank you, *Charity.*"

"Th-thank you."

"You're welcome. Now, can I have that ride?"

ZIPPING ALONG with the top down, Adam all big and rangy and beyond-belief handsome beside her, Charity wasn't sure whether to laugh or to cry.

He'd *kissed* her.

Bought her a car.

What did it mean? Was it truly just a friendly gesture? And what about that kiss? Talk about confusing!

"Turn here," he said, squinting against the bright fall sun.

"Why?" she asked.

"Because that's the way to the next installment of my apology surprise."

"I think you've already done way more than necessary," she said. "And besides, I'm partially to blame, too. I could've just agreed to go out with you. You know, strictly to get that shrink off your back. So if you still want me to be your pretend date, I will. For medicinal purposes."

"That sounds good," he said. "It'll be like a scientific thing."

"Absolutely."

For the next thirty minutes they rode in companionable silence—well, silence save for the Velvet Revolver CD blaring on the awesome sound system.

Autumn colors and smells were in full swing. A wake of red and gold leaves swirled behind them. The air was flavored with sweet wood smoke from hearth fires built to ward off the evening chill.

Adam kept giving directions, and she kept following until the area again grew familiar. "Are we heading for your sister-in-law's restaurant?"

"Maybe."

"Adam, this is too much. Her place is pricey." Gracie Logue, Beau's wife, was a world-renowned chef. After barely surviving a nightmare with her psycho ex-husband, she was now living the good life. Amazing job. Enchanted marriage. Plus, she'd been on dozens of TV shows and won so many awards for her culinary skills, her hubby built an addition on to their home—right alongside the new nursery—to accommodate them all.

"And you're not worth it?"

"I didn't say that," she said with a grin and flip of her flirty new hair. In this car, she not only felt pretty, but confident. As if maybe she really did have a shot at landing a great catch like Adam. Even better, if her luck held, she might land Adam himself.

While the sun set, they dined on black bean soup,

grilled filet mignon, wilted watercress and horserad-ish-whipped potatoes on a patio with radiant heaters and a breathtaking view of Mount Hood. Upping the fairy-tale atmosphere were the little things. Such as their fingers brushing when she'd handed Adam the salt; the way, when she'd said her feet were cold, he'd gallantly lifted them onto his lap and used his fingers to warm her toes.

She wasn't sure how it'd happened, but tonight had to have marked a changing point in their relationship. Sure, they'd still be great friends, but now there'd be that added spark she'd long dreamed of them sharing.

Over a dessert of cranberry-apple crumble with Irish oatmeal crust, Adam asked, "You ready to hammer out the details?"

"Of what?" Charity asked, still dreamy over the unexpected—magical—night's course. Chez Bon was a million miles from Ziggy's, and the fact that Adam had wanted to share the place with her made her feel like the most special woman in the world.

"You know." Adam reached over the low candle and flower arrangement in the table's center to steal a bite of her dessert.

"Hey!" she complained, pulling the plate closer to her and hopefully out of his reach. "I'm still eating that."

"Sorry. I'm starving. Gracie's a great cook and all, but I'm more a meat-and-potatoes guy."

"We had meat and potatoes."

"Yeah, but not enough."

Rolling her eyes, she shoved her half-finished dessert toward him. "Here. Knock yourself out."

"Cool. Then maybe we can stop by McDonald's on the way home. I'd kill for a Double Quarter Pounder with cheese."

"Thanks," she said with a half grin.

"Sure, but for what?"

"Sucking every shred of romance from this beautiful setting." A local guitarist sang folk tunes and some of the other couples dining on the patio had started to dance in the moonlight.

"They might be feeling romance vibes," he said. "But not us, right? I like you—a lot. But you know what I mean. That's why we have to work out the details of this whole pretend-dating thing, just so we don't accidentally have a for-real date or anything along those lines."

Charity leaned forward, elbows on the table. "You're kidding, right?"

"Me? Kid on a topic as serious as romance?" He laughed. "When I lost Angela, I threw away the key to—" He pressed his palm to his chest. "Don't get me wrong. I still love people. My family—even you. Just not *that* way."

"Sure," she said, suddenly nauseous from the rich food. Or maybe it was Adam's ridiculous speech making her sick? Had he forgotten kissing her? Had he forgotten giving her a car as an apology gift? The way their fingers brushed while passing each other the salt? How he'd warmed her cold feet?

"So?" he asked. "Ready to hit the road?"

Shell-shocked, she nodded.

Charity was just pushing back her chair when Gracie, Adam's sister-in-law and Chez Bon's head chef and half owner, bustled over. She was six months' pregnant and she looked radiant, with a contentment Gracie feared she'd never know. "How was everything?" she asked.

"I'm still hungry," Adam complained.

Gracie swatted him over the head with a dishrag.

"It was delicious," Charity said. "Best meal I've had since the last time you fed me."

"Wonderful," Gracie said. "I'm glad at least one of you enjoyed it. Although, Charity, Beau tells me you and Sam are getting to be quite the item. Maybe next time I'll see you two lovebirds at my best table?"

"You all right?" Gracie asked Adam when he choked on his last swig of coffee. Patting his back, to Charity she said, "Beau said you two look darling together. You and Sam, that is. This oaf of a brother-in-law of mine you're with tonight is strictly *friend* material."

Oh, now that made Charity feel better—not!

What was she supposed to say to a thing like that? And what had given Beau the outrageous idea that she and Sam were a couple? Sure, they'd been out for a few casual lunches at the Subway down the street from the office, but those had been no big deal.

Nothing like this night during which every bone in her body screamed this was *it*. The night Adam finally got his head out of his rear and realized how great the two of them could be as so much more than friends.

"Well," Gracie said, again to Charity, as if Adam wasn't even at the table. "I know you have a long drive ahead of you in that darling new car. Gillian told me all about it. Plus, I imagine you'll want to get home early enough to call Sam to have him wish you good-night."

"Gracie," Charity said, placing her napkin on the table in front of her, "I think you've got the wrong idea about me and Sam. He's just—"

"You don't have to pretend things are casual between you on my account," Gracie said. "Beau's good at sniffing out interoffice romances."

Adam snorted.

"Did you say something?" Gracie asked, hand on his shoulder.

"Bug," Adam said. "Hand me your keys and I'll get the car."

"I can do it myself," Charity said.

"But I already said I'll do it for you."

At the intensity behind his dark stare, Charity's stomach did a nervous flutter. Could he have made the request to be gentlemanly? Or had Gracie's rambling about Sam actually upset him? At the very least, sparking his competitive edge where his office rival was concerned. Just in case, she, as demurely as possible, reached into her purse for the keys, handing them across the table, trying with all her might to ignore hot tingles when their fingers brushed yet again.

"Thanks," he said, eyes suddenly bright. "I've been itching to get my hands on this baby's wheel. See how she performs on that curvy section between here and Johnson Avenue."

Pop. Charity's mood fell like a deflated balloon. She should've known Adam's request hadn't been about chivalry, but trying out her ride.

"Let me know how things go with Sam," Gracie said. "If you all need a place to hold your engagement party, I'd be honored if you'd let me host it here."

"Engagement party?" Adam snorted. "I don't think anyone's to that stage yet. Come on, Bug. Let's go get that burger."

"Love you, Adam!" Gracie called as her brother-in-law hustled Charity off into the night. Fingers crossed, she whispered, "Love you, too, Charity. It might look like Adam's an impossible catch, but believe you me, with all three Logue women, plus Daddy Logue on the case, it's only a matter of time before Adam's begging you to head down the aisle!"

Chapter Four

Adam pulled up beside his truck in the office lot. He'd driven them here from the restaurant and Bug— Charity—had climbed out and now stood beside him, holding out her hand for the keys. He handed them over. Despite his best efforts, it'd been a twisted night. Ever since kissing her this afternoon, there'd been weirdness between them. Why had he done it? Why couldn't he stop thinking about trying it again? "Guess this is it."

"Yep," she said, slipping her keys into her pocket, then yawning.

"You're tired. How about we leave my car here and I drive you home."

"I don't have a problem driving," she said with a funny smile. "And how come that statement smacks of you looking for another excuse to get behind the wheel of my new car? And what happens once we get to my condo? You inviting yourself to sleep over?"

"How come lately you're always thinking the

worst of me?" Lips pressed tight, shoving his hands into his pockets, he said, "I apologized for being an ass about you wanting to have a baby. I gave you a freakin' car. What more do I have to do to show you how sorry I am?"

Taking his hands from his pockets, he cupped her slight shoulders. What was it about this transformation of hers that had him all the time wanting to touch her? It wasn't normal. He wasn't always touching his guy friends. "This is going to sound corny as hell, but, Bug—Charity—you're pretty much all I have. You know, aside from my family."

She looked down. "That's sweet, Adam, but—"

"Dammit, Bug, I don't wanna be sweet, I want things back the way they were. I like hanging out with you every night. You're good company."

"But don't you get it?" she said, eyes all shimmery, as though she might cry. Bug, cry? He didn't know it was possible. "I'm thirty-five years old, Adam. I'm tired of *hanging around.* I want what Gillian and Joe have."

Adam snorted. "Don't we all? What I couldn't do with a spare hundred mil or so."

"Quit joking around. I'm not talking about the money, but their relationship. What they share—their love—it's priceless. Same with Beau and Gracie, and Caleb and Allie. Don't you ever want that for yourself? Don't you ever find yourself wanting more?"

What was he supposed to say to that?

His sister and two brothers had hit the jackpot when it came to love. What they all shared was so close to perfection, that from the outside, looking in, it didn't even seem real. No one could actually be that happy, could they?

He'd once been. A long time ago.

But then, hell, come to think of it, he had been before this fuss with Bug, too. They weren't...like romantic or anything, but what they shared worked. They made a great team.

So why not go for broke and make it more?

Suddenly hot despite the cold night air, he turned his back on her and walked away. "I'd better get going. It's late."

"Wait!" she called, chasing him to the driver's side of his truck, her new high heels making a weird sexy clacking that echoed through the empty underground garage. He turned around, watching her hair bounce—not to mention other parts of her anatomy he hadn't heretofore noticed her having been amply blessed. "I'll help."

"Help me get home?" he asked, mouth strangely dry at the sight of her flushed cheeks.

"No. With your dates. You know, with how your shrink says you have to go out. I'll be your unofficial girl."

"But I thought you had better things to do now that you're looking for a husband."

"I'll do both," she said. "Sam's been showing

interest, but who's to say I can't go out on early dates with him, then late ones with you?"

Just the thought of her being with that guy brought Adam's blood to an instant boil. "No."

"Excuse me?"

"Thanks for the offer, but in order for this to be convincing, I think it'd be best if you saw only me— at least until the shrink pronounces me cured."

"Oh."

"I know that's asking a lot," he said. "But surely it won't take too long. A month or three—tops."

"Um, sure. That'd probably be all right."

"Good."

"So then what do I tell Sam next time he asks me out? That is, assuming he does."

"Oh, he will. And all you have to do is tell him you're with me."

"Am I? With you?"

"Um, sure. I mean…" He scrunched his nose. Was this one of those pass/fail women tests? How was he supposed to answer an asinine question like that?

A blue Impala revved by. The smelly exhaust only further befuddled his mind.

"Sorry I even brought it up," she said, eyes all shimmery again.

"Good grief…" He pulled her into a hug. "No apology necessary. Besides, if anyone's sorry, it's me. I shouldn't even be dragging you into this." He kissed the top of her head. Had she always smelled this good? All sugary and sexy-sweet? "Promise," he said, pushing Bug slightly back, just far enough so he could see into her big, wet eyes. "I'll make this worth your while."

"How? Because I don't need any more cars or—"

Lord only knew why, but he stopped her infernal questioning with a kiss. No biggee. Just a peck between friends. "It's late. Go home. Get into bed. We'll hammer out the details *mañana*."

"Okay," she said, hands pressed to his chest, making her seem suddenly small and him so big and protective. Kind of the way he used to feel before losing Angela. He never thought he could feel that way again. Did this mean there was hope for him to eventually have a decent future? Or was he deluding himself?

"Come on," he said. "I'll tuck you in your car."

She let him lead her there, open the door, help her in and fasten her seat belt.

"Want me to follow you home?" he asked.

"No, thanks. I'm good."

"Just checking. If we're going to be an official item, even if it is just pretend, I can't have you ditching me for lack of manners."

"WELL, WELL, Mr. Logue," Adam's shrink said Thursday afternoon. "You certainly have been a busy beaver. I only asked for one date and here you've had three. All with different women."

Adam shrugged. "No biggee."

"How did it feel?"

Kissing Bug? Holding her? Catching whiffs of that sexy new lotion?

"I'm sorry," he said with a shake of his head, squashing the memory along with the stone in the pit of his gut. He cleared his throat, squirmed in his chair. "Could you please rephrase the question?"

"Once again entering the land of the living—how did that feel? Were the dates fun? Aggravating? Did any of the women make you feel especially glad to be alive?" She scribbled something on his chart. "Let's go through each date—starting with the swimsuit model. Give me the first, one-word description that pops into your head."

"Flat."

"Hmm… Very interesting. And the legal secretary?"

"Manila folder."

"That's two words."

"Isn't it more like a compound word?"

She nodded, consulting his chart. "I'll let it slide. And your co-worker? Charity Caldwell?"

"Pears."

"Excuse me?"

"She got this new lotion from her sister, a gift from Victoria's Secret. It's the damnedest thing. The lotion, I mean. Smells like pears—only sweeter."

"I see." Scribble, scribble.

From the table beside him, Adam took a plastic snow globe of the Vegas strip and gave it a shake.

Pretty. Maybe he and Bug could trek down to Vegas someday.

His shrink asked, "Do you have plans to ask any of these women out again, or would you prefer to select a fresh batch?"

"Charity. For sure, I'll see her again. In fact, we're supposed to have dinner tonight."

"Wonderful. At a restaurant?"

"Nah. Her apartment."

"Ahh…" She raised her eyebrows as she wrote. "That's a relatively big step. A woman cooking for you in her home."

"I'll help. I don't expect her to wait on me."

That really sent the shrink into a writing frenzy. Was helpfulness bad or good? God, he'd give anything for some kind of gauge as to how this appointment was going. So far, he felt as though he was playing it cool. Giving the shrink everything she wanted, but—

"In the midst of your suddenly swinging new social life," she said, "have you had many thoughts of Angela Jacobs?"

"No."

Up went the doc's eyebrows. "That was fast. None at all? No comparing her with the new women in your life? Rating how they stack up against her?"

"No."

Scribble, scribble, scribble.

"This has been a highly productive session,

Mr. Logue. I really do think we're making progress, don't you?"

"In what way?"

She beamed. "In *every* way. See you next week."

"You should've heard her," Adam complained at Bug's that night. He sat on the kitchen counter while she scurried like a rooster, trying to make some fancy supper. Beef stroganoff, if he remembered correctly. "All up into my business. Making me talk and talk about all three of my supposed dates."

"What'd you tell her?" Bug asked, stirring a bubbling pot of egg noodles.

"Everything." He laughed. "She made me go on and on. All in all, I'd say it was excruciating." Kind of like sitting here, watching his Bug get all sweaty from steam. And where in the hell had she gotten this latest get-up she had on? Low-riding faded jeans and a skintight pink T-shirt riding up her abdomen, giving him teasing little glimpses of her taut stomach. And what was that sparkle? Right there—"Whoa!" He'd tried so hard to catch a glimpse that he fell off the counter.

"You okay?" she asked, back to stirring the meat sauce. She'd put her new blond hair in a stubby ponytail, but even that was somehow different with escape strands wisping around her cheeks.

"Yeah. Sure. Just trying to figure out what you did to your stomach."

"You mean this?" She raised her shirt, flashing him a shiny new belly ring. "Steph took me to get it. She said guys really go for this sort of thing. It's like a fishing lure. And since… Well, you know, I'm trying to get out there and date, I figured why not go for it."

"Sure," he said with a gulp, wishing, praying she'd lower her shirt so he'd lose his ridiculous urge to lunge at her belly with all the aplomb of a large-mouthed bass. "Makes sense."

"So? What do you think?"

"Strictly from a male *friend's* point of view?" he asked. Had his voice come out as strained as it felt considering the amount of stress her question put him under?

"Of course. What other views other than *friendly* ones would you be having?" She winked before dumping a bunch of flour into the pot. It clouded, and she coughed and laughed, stepping back from the stove to wave her hand in front of her face.

"You all right?" he asked, patting her back.

She giggled. "Uh-huh. Who knew flour explodes?"

"Here," he said, grabbing her wooden spoon. "Let me help."

He took over stirring for her, damned grateful at having a safe place to hide the party going on behind his fly. How many hundreds of times had he been over here? Yet never once had this happened.

Well… The other night when he'd caught Bug in that sexy negligee, but that was different. This was just cooking. No way should he be aroused doing nothing but watching Bug stir.

He glanced over his shoulder to catch her take a salad from the fridge, then put it on the already-set table. The table he'd never once seen draped in a cloth, but that now sported not only nonchipped dishes and matching silverware, but flowers and a flickering candle. "What's up with the fancy stuff?"

"I just figured in case your shrink wants specifics, this'll add a more realistic flair to your report."

"Good thinking," he said, giving the simmering contents of the pot a few obligatory swipes. "Want me to pop the cork on that wine I brought?"

"It's not twist-off?" she asked with another of her new winks.

"Ha, ha."

She leaned over to get the wine from the fridge, in the process, treating him to the backside of her hip-hugging jeans. Was she wearing pink thong panties? He swallowed hard.

She set the wine on the counter, fishing in her junk drawer for the corkscrew.

"It's in the silverware drawer," he said.

"What's it doing there?"

"Last time I helped with dishes, I think I stashed it there."

"But you know I keep it in the junk drawer."

"I know, but the game was on and—"

On her way to the silverware drawer, she swatted his chest. "You're like a bad little boy shirking his chores."

Corkscrew in hand, she tried doing the simple task, but couldn't.

"Here," he said, stepping up behind her, hands on top of hers on the cool, slick bottle. "Let me try."

For the first time that night, her confidence looked shaken. For just a second she was back to the old Bug. The one who claimed insecurity about everything from her looks to her effect—or lack thereof—on men. "You don't need to worry, you know?"

"A-about what?" Trapped in the circle of his arms, she looked up, in the process, unwittingly bringing her lips to a perfect kissing level.

"Your wine-opening skills." He grinned. "Anything, really. I don't know what's got into you lately, but believe me—strictly from a guy friend's point of view—you've got it going on."

"Th-thanks." She swallowed hard.

"Any time."

"Ready to eat?" Charity asked, desperate to do anything other than stand in the circle of Adam's arms. Did he have any idea what this closeness did to her? Because it wasn't her skills—or lack thereof—that currently had her worried, but the erratic beat of her heart!

"Sure. Want me to help get everything on the table?"

"Please." Together, brushing shoulders and hips in the cramped kitchen, they put noodles and sauce, salad, wine and rolls on the table Steph had coached her to beautifully set for two. Only once they sat, and Adam began heaping both of their plates with the lumpy, clunky white concoction Steph assured her would be not only easy to fix but taste divine, Charity began to worry maybe she'd overdone it with the flour.

Adam took the first bite. "Mmm. Good," he said, deadpan expression not giving any clue as to how he really felt. "Wine?" he asked.

"Yes, please."

While he poured, she took a bite only to prompt-ly spit it out, then rinse her mouth with tart red wine. "Blech. I can't believe you actually swal-lowed this stuff. What happened? I did everything Steph told me to."

"It's not that bad," he said, forking another bite.

"Yes," she said, hand on his, preventing him from making a potentially lethal mistake. "It is."

He cautiously eyed her, almost as if checking to see if it really was okay to admit her first stab at making a fancy meal had flopped. Good grief, how did she expect to feed a baby when she couldn't even prepare a meal for herself? Let alone the child's po-tential father.

"Go ahead," she said. "You won't hurt my feelings if you tell the truth."

"You sure? After all, you did go to an awful lot of trouble."

I'm sure," she said, pushing back her chair before

snatching the stroganoff bowl, then heading for the disposal.

"Got any butter?" he asked right behind her.

"I think. Check the compartment in the fridge."

He did and found half a stick. He melted it in the microwave, then drenched the noodles in it.

"Good idea," she said, reaching for garlic salt. "Add some of this."

He did. "Got parmesan?"

She checked, found half a can, then reached around him to shake it on, for once leaning into him instead of away. Up close, he smelled way better than dinner. Like his leather jacket and an autumn blend of fallen leaves and rain and the year's first frost.

Back at the table, they split the noodles and doled out salad she'd already tossed with Italian dressing.

"This is good," he said.

"Sorry about the first disaster."

"Truly, it wasn't *that* bad."

She gave him a stop-joshing-me look, which resulted in him busting out laughing. She soon followed until she was laughing so hard, she cried.

"It tasted like wallpaper paste with beefy nuggets," he said.

"No—like that poi Franks made us eat at the birthday luau his wife threw him last summer."

"Eeuw. I'd forgotten that nightmare. Thanks a lot. And, yes, hate to say it, but your stuff was a wee bit worse."

"No way was it as bad as that gray goop in a bowl."

"Yes, way."

Making a growling sound, she wadded up her napkin and tossed it at him.

He caught it midair, then leaned over the table, tossing the oversize scrap of yellow cloth around her neck. "With this lei, I hereby name you Miss Worst Cook of the Year."

"Thank you," she said, taking his joke in stride. "And for you being such a fearless taste-tester to have been able to make that determination…" She stood, too, slinging her napkin around his neck. "With this lei, I name you Mr. Lucky."

"Why?" he asked. Her arms around his neck, her breasts pressed his chest through her suddenly-too-thin T-shirt. Her nipples, unaccustomed to company, instantly, exquisitely, hardened. Her stomach tightened, making it hard to breathe. "Am I lucky because I just got lei'd?"

She licked her lips. "I, um, was thinking you were lucky because you survived the meal."

He shook his head, grinned. "Let's get back to the lei part."

"What about it?"

"Wanna?"

"Lei you?"

He nodded, leaned forward just far enough to brush his lips against hers. "Just for practice. You know, to authenticate the evening."

Chapter Five

"I don't know," Charity said, joining him as they stepped around the small table, close enough for her to tell by the size of his erection he wasn't fooling. "You really think sleeping together's a good idea? What would your shrink say?"

He kissed her again. This time long and leisurely with a tantalizing sweep of his wine-flavored tongue. "You really care what she thinks?"

Heart racing, she said, "I wouldn't want to impede your healing process."

"Then, yeah, I need lei-ing right away. *Please.*" He slid his hands into her back pockets, using their location to his advantage by pressing their hips even closer. "Lord Almighty, Bug, what have you done to me? I'm on fire for you, girl."

Meeting him for another spellbinding kiss, she said, "All I did was a cook a lousy dinner."

"Then you need to start doing it more often. Hell, you should've done it years ago."

"So then, what you're essentially saying is the only thing that kept this from happening all those other nights we were together was edible food?"

He nodded, planting a string of hot, sexy kisses up her throat. "Uh-huh."

"Okay, so if we did head for the bedroom— strictly for practice, seeing how we're both probably a little rusty. Then, what?"

"You talk too much," he said, nibbling her earlobe.

"I agree, but, Adam, seriously, if we do this, what happens at the office tomorrow?"

"Who cares?" He lifted her, caveman-style, to the sofa, then eased on top of her, creating the most amazing pressure and heat that drove out all sanity, leaving room in her blazing body for nothing but more of his special brand of pleasure.

"Sam might care."

Like a scratched record, Adam pushed himself off of her, then stood, staring down at her with his hands on his hips. "You seriously didn't just say that idiot's name while here I am, putting my best moves on you?"

"He's hardly an idiot," she said, pushing herself upright. "Especially since Franks gave him the office Top Gun award last year for having successfully completed the most take-downs of any of us. That is, aside from Caleb, but he's in a class all his own."

"I'm gone," Adam said with a disgusted snort.

"But, Adam…" She stood, brushed hair that'd escaped her once-neat ponytail from her face.

"Listen up," he said, hand on the doorknob. "I want no mention of that slimeball in my presence. Especially not while I'm kissing you. Got it?"

She couldn't help but giggle at his roar.

"What's funny? Because I'm dead serious."

"Oh, I can tell," she said.

"Then you agree?"

"To what?" she innocently asked.

"Never mention that guy's name around me again. Especially when I'm kissing you."

"Who says you're going to be kissing me again?" She raised her chin.

"Who says? Me." After storming to where she stood, he placed one hand on the small of her back, the other he slid into her hair, cupping her head, kissing her hard, deep, dizzy until she'd have agreed to anything he'd said—especially to never think of any man besides him.

"THIS SWEET AND SOUR pork is awesome," Adam said around seven the next night from his usual seat on Bug's sofa. He was surprised when she'd invited him over again. But then, before they'd started dating, he'd been over most every night. On the surface, nothing was different between them, so how come on the inside, everything had changed? How come just looking at Bug brought on a rush of confusion? Emotionally, he was all over the map. Attracted, possessive, turned-on, scared to lose her. More scared of never having had her. "Good call. We haven't had Chinese in a while."

Bug was in the kitchen, making herself a plate. He'd offered to do it for her, carefully avoiding any and all physical or eye contact, but thankfully, she'd declined.

If only she'd passed on wearing another sexy outfit!

This time, she was killing him with baby-blue sweats.

Sounded safe enough, only they were that new cut-off style that looked as though someone had hacked them off at the ankle. Bug had rolled them midway up her sexy, still-tanned calves. Even worse, they rode low on her hips, and her tight white T-shirt rode high, resulting in a bared strip of belly and that sparkling lure he wanted to bite—bad. So he'd looked down, only to be faced with the sight of adorable red-tipped toes he wanted to suck—bad. So then he'd looked up, to her face. Only her T-shirt had an ultra-low collar that'd left her chest and throat exposed. And she wore her hair down, all wild and messy, filling him with crazy urges to use his fingers to comb it back, then kiss every bit of soft, pear-scented skin he'd exposed.

Swallowing hard, Adam reached for the remote.

Last night had nearly been a disaster of his own making. Not that he wouldn't have loved every minute of sleeping with Bug, but putting the moves on your best friend wasn't cool. Didn't matter that Bug had transformed herself into an exotic creature he now thought of as *Buglicious,* he had far too much respect for her to take advantage of her in that way.

She deserved better than sofa surfing. She deserved it all. Cute little house. That baby and husband she wanted all tied up with a neat, white picket fence.

In him, all she'd ever find was a guy trapped in the past. He'd promised, with Angela dying in his arms, to love her forever, and by God, that was what he'd do. And seeing how he already had her in his heart, it'd be kinda hard to let another woman in—not that he was even considering such a thing with Bug. Just that he couldn't in good conscience sleep with her without in turn loving her—not as a friend, but girlfriend. Wife.

Scowling, hand to his chest in a feeble attempt to stave off fiery heartburn, with his free hand he reached for the remote. "Sports, documentary or slasher movie, if I can find one?"

"I was thinking," she said, parking her sweet self entirely too close to him on the sofa. "Maybe we should try a night without TV."

"You mean, play video games instead? Love it. X-Box or PlayStation II?"

"No games, either."

"Then what?" he asked, hoping he hadn't been caught staring at her perfectly rounded—

"Well… Seeing how this is supposed to be a date, I thought we might try something new. You know, like having a discussion."

"On what? All we ever talk about is TV or video games."

"That's my point. If you happen to let that fact slip to your shrink, she'll be on you like fly on stink. Adam, you've got to be smarter than her." She tapped her temple. "*Really* fake her out."

"I see your point," he said, nodding in sudden understanding. And relief. He could fully give in to his mysterious new feelings toward his best friend, and in doing so, would only be furthering himself in his therapy. Kind of like that thing actors or writers do with deep character immersion. "Nice. Thanks, Bug. I appreciate you watching my back on this one." He shook his head and grinned. "I never would've seen this coming, but you're right. Her being a woman and all, she's probably into that touchy-feely stuff." Oops, judging by the suddenly stricken look on his Bug's face, looks like he'd screwed up again. "Not that you aren't all woman," he said, backpedaling as fast as he could. "Just that you're more fun than most women. You don't have the usual goofy female baggage."

Deeply engrossed in her sweet and sour pork, she didn't say a word. Was that a good or bad thing?

"I've always liked that about you," he said. "Lack of a need to incessantly hash over the minutia of our lives is a turn-on. Not that I am turned on by you, but you know what I mean."

Still chewing. She wouldn't even look his way.

And she'd gone all tense—something he sensed more than saw—but what was he supposed to do about it?

"Okay, let's discuss," he said with an admittedly cheesy grin, willing to try anything to get himself out of her doghouse. "What'll it be? Movies? Food? No—I've got it. Bugs. Give me some fantastic fact no one but you would know."

"I'd rather not," she said, reaching to the coffee table for her Coke can.

"Oh, come on. Dazzle me. Better yet. Give me a true or false quiz. You throw something out, then I'll guess if it's true or false."

She rolled her eyes.

"I'm trying here," he said. "I don't even put this much effort into making a real date happy, yet look at me, dancing around like some dork-ass circus dog in an apparently futile attempt to please you."

"Sorry," she said, setting her can and barely touched food on the table. "Guess I'm still kind of stuck back on your speech about me not being a girly girl. I've done everything I could to hopefully be more attractive as a woman—not only to you, but to other guys, as well. Marrying-type guys. But it looks like nothing's ever going to work." Her eyes welled up, and this time, instead of her just looking like she was going to cry, she really did. "W-when my twin brother died, so did my dad. I thought I could bring him back by becoming my brother. And I did. B-but in the process, I lost myself. And if I can't find a man, how am I going to have a baby? Will I even make a good mom? And if I am a good mom, will I then be a crappy marshal?"

"Oh, honey, you'll make a great mom and could never be anything but a great marshal." He pulled her into his arms, but when that didn't seem like enough, he dragged her onto his lap, rocking her while she cried. "And you're doing a phenomenal job of looking like every guy's fantasy. Good lord, woman, why else do you think I'd've tried every trick in the book to sleep with you last night? As for that thing with your dad…" He pushed her gently back, brushing her tears with the pads of his thumbs. "What you did for him was amazing. You've told me about your brother, but this is the first time you've said a word about you trying to *be* your brother." Hands on either side of her dear face, forcing her to meet his stare, he said, "That's crazy. No one can replace another loved one. I'm pissed at your parents for not recognizing the fact that you were trying. But that's in the past now. Tonight, this second, you're all woman. Hot, sexy, blowing my mind. And if you don't believe me…" He glanced at his bulging fly.

Following his gaze, she laughed.

"Think that's funny?" Laughing along with her, cupping the back of her head to kiss her forehead, he said, "It hurts. And it's your fault. So stop being so damned gorgeous, okay?"

She nodded, then blew him away by snuggling against him. Snuggling! Friends don't snuggle.

Speaking of which, what was his problem? Having to further adjust his fly while snuggling wasn't such a smooth move, either. The fact that she'd confided in him about her dad was an even bigger turn-on than her makeover. So why couldn't he reciprocate? She deserved so much more from him. Why couldn't he open himself up and give?

"What's happening to us?" he moaned into his Bug's pear-scented hair. "It's like we're still friends, but not. There's weirdness."

"I know," she said, voice muffled from where she'd curled herself against his shoulder.

"This is all my fault. I should've never asked you to date me—even pretend dating is too big a strain on our—" What? Relationship? He shuddered to have even thought the word. Yet when it came right down to it, that's what he and Bug shared. They were a unit. Tight. Only they weren't supposed to be a kissing unit. Just friendly. And all because of that damned shrink, he'd blown it.

He swiped his hand through his hair. Was it suddenly hot in here or had there been too much MSG in his sweet and sour pork?

SATURDAY MORNING Charity vowed to shoot whoever was banging on her door at five in the morning.

She peered through the peephole, and there was Adam. Grinning. Proudly holding up a drink carrier with two large coffees and a sack of doughnuts.

"Rise and shine," he said with a wag of the sack. "I've got great news."

She opened the door, stepping aside to let him in.

"You're not going to believe this," he said, parking himself on the sofa, his food and drink on the coffee table. The fragrant java made Charity's stomach growl. "But I managed to wrangle us a couple seats on my pal Wallace's deep-sea fishing boat."

"Huh?" she asked, sitting beside him, glad she'd fallen asleep in her sweats and T-shirt instead of that stupid silk nightgown her sister insisted she wear in case of pop-in visits like this. "Since when do you have a friend named Wallace who fishes?"

"Remember? He was an expert witness for the state on that drug case we worked back in 2003."

She shook her head, helped herself to a doughnut. "Refresh my memory. Why'd the state need an expert fishing witness?"

He graced her with his most disgusted sigh. "I can't believe you forgot a case like that. The defendant killed narcs by using them as trolling bait. Remember how my pal Wallace gave the court a lesson in hook sizes, and the probability of how long it'd take a guy to either drown or be eaten?"

Charity shuddered. It was probably for the best she'd forgotten. Talk about nightmarish images. "Mind telling me how any of that landed you on my doorstep while it's still dark outside?"

"Hello?" he said around a bite of doughnut. "Free seats? A day spent fishing? Ring any bells?"

Leaning her head against the sofa, she moaned. "Please tell me this is all just a bad dream."

He grinned. "Just as soon as I can find you some shoes, we're out of here. I even got us a lunch. Your favorite—bologna and mustard on white."

She rolled her eyes. Steph, her healthy diet coach, would love that!

"I don't know," Charity said. "Fishing's never really been my thing."

"Then you can just admire my fishing prowess."

"Gee, that sounds fun."

He winked, vaulting her stomach into the stratosphere. How come when here she was, fresh off a night spent convincing herself she'd be better off without the guy, he went and pulled a stunt like this? Thoroughly annoying, but in such a cute way.

Maybe there was hope for the two of them, after all? Maybe she'd been wrong to plan on throwing in the towel on this whole dating charade? Maybe, if she were really lucky, they wouldn't spend the day fishing, but gazing out at the water, then deep into each other's eyes.

"Think we can take your car to the docks?" he asked, her sneakers in hand. "I've been dying to get my hands back on that little beauty."

While Adam headed to the kitchen to stock up on

Cokes, she snorted. Yep, they'd get to all of those romantic *maybes*—right after pigs learned to fly!

"WHAT'S WRONG?" Charity asked Adam about an hour into their cruise through Tillamook Bay. They were fishing for Chinook, and though she'd never been all that keen on the sport, it was shaping up to be a gorgeous day. Bright sun sparkled the choppy water. The brisk wind and fresh sea air were invigorating. The thought of landing a sixty-pound Chinook salmon *waaay* exciting. "This whole trip was your idea, but you're looking a tad green in the gills." She snort-laughed, elbowing his ribs. "Get it? Gills? I crack myself up."

"Do you have to be so loud?" he complained.

"Do you have to be so whiny? What's the problem?"

"I'm sick. Seeing how you're suddenly all girly now, where's your sensitivity?"

"Aw," she said with a grin, patting his head. "Poor baby. Want me to get you a yummy mustard and bologna sandwich? Can't you just smell that bologna? Feel all that yummy fat coating your—"

Blech! Adam yakked over the side of the boat.

Oops.

Chapter Six

"Sweetie," Charity said, trying to keep hold of her trolling rod while at the same time rubbing Adam's back. "I'm sorry. I was just messing with you for waking me up so early. I didn't think you were really that sick."

"Yeah, well, I am," he snapped.

"Hold my pole," she said. "Let me see if I can round up some Sprite and crackers."

He shook his head. "That's okay. Just let me die in peace."

She rolled her eyes, but all the same helped him to a vinyl-covered bench. "Try not to think about it," she said. "And look at the horizon. I've heard that helps."

"Nothing's going to help. I told you, I'm dy—" He tossed his cookies again. Or in his case, eight doughnuts and coffee.

She rubbed his back for a while, but then her pole suddenly hunched over.

"Hey!" the hairy guy standing next to her hollered. "You got one. And from the looks of it, he's a monster!"

More than two hours later she'd reeled in a fifty-eight-pound Chinook salmon. By the cheers and adulation of the six guys on board—not counting Adam, who'd gone below—you'd have thought she'd reeled in a flat-screen TV. Never had she felt so important. Just think, it hadn't taken landing a mastermind crook, but a massive fish.

Early that evening, back at the dock, she posed for pictures then made taxidermy arrangements—no way was she just going to eat the beauty. She wanted him around for all time. Bragging rights this good couldn't be bought! Even better, Captain Wallace asked her permission to use her photo on his charter service's Web page. Of course, she agreed.

If Adam had told her she'd have this much fun fishing, she never would've believed him. But not only had she liked it, she was great at it! Could she do that with dating and parenting, too?

Charity went in search of Adam, and found him in the fetal position, huddled under a rough wool blanket on a lower berth across from the boat's smelly bathroom.

Boy, was she a great friend, or what? Leaving him down here, miserable all day while she'd had the time of her life. And here she supposedly loved him. Or did she? Was the fact that she'd just abandoned him like this—despite the increased sexual tension of the past few days—a sign that they were nothing more than pals?

She put her hand on his shoulder. "Adam, sweetie? Time to wake up."

"Hey," he said, sleepy-eyed with an algae-colored complexion. "You catch anything?"

"Only the biggest fish of the day. Fifty-eight pounds."

"Damn," he said, voice scratchy and weak. "I'm impressed. High-five."

She held her hand up so he could slap it.

"That's great," he said, "So how did that make you feel, wrestling him in?"

"Truthfully," she said with sheepish grin, "like I was on top of the world. As if I could accomplish anything I set my mind to."

"Mission accomplished."

"Huh?" She scratched her head. "You planned this whole thing?"

He cast her that slow grin of his that she so adored. "Right down to having the diver put a gorgeous fish on your line."

"You'd do that for little ole me?" she teased, batting her eyelashes, knowing full well she'd caught that fish on her own.

"Heck, yeah—despite the fact that I got zero nursing from you."

"Sorry," she said, brushing the hair back from his clammy forehead. "Guess I just got lost in the moment."

"Cool," he said. "Then it was worth it."

"What? I thought you got our seats for free?"

Captain Wallace clumped down the boat's stairs. "Good, good, I see our sickie's finally back to the land of the livin'."

"Almost," Adam said.

"Good, good. Well, I hate to bother you, kind sir, seeing how you haven't had a pole in the water all day, but I need to settle up or the wifey'll have my hide. She does all the accounting, and with fuel prices being what they are…"

"It's not a problem," Adam said, reaching into his back pocket for his wallet, then pulling out a wad of cash. "Here you go."

The captain counted out three hundred in twenties, then folded the bills and handed Adam a prewritten receipt. "Pleasure doing business with you, son. Hope your next trip, you stock up on Dramamine instead of bologna."

"Eeuw." Adam winced. "Please, don't even say the word."

"I STILL CAN'T believe you forked over that much money just to try to make me feel good about myself," Charity said, tucking Adam into her bed. He'd insisted he'd rather recuperate at her condo than his apartment. And seeing how sweet he'd been to her and how she'd abandoned him at his time of need, she'd agreed. "What even made you think up such a thing?"

"Long story," he said, propping one of her prized antique feather pillows behind his still-greenish head.

"We've kinda got all night," she said, snatching a pillow for herself so she could recline next to him. She smelled like fish and badly needed a shower, but for the moment, nothing sounded better than lying beside Adam. "Come on, spill it."

"Hmm…" he said, a partial spark back in his eyes. "Seems to me the last time I made that demand, I got hurled into a recliner."

"That was different," she said, cheeks reddening at the thought of how dangerously good it'd felt with him on top of her, pinning her to the floor.

"How so?" he teased.

She landed a playful swat to his shoulder. "Just get on with the story."

"All right," he said with a big sigh. "But only because you've browbeaten me into it."

She gave him a dirty look.

"Okay, you know how my mom died when I was just a kid, right?"

"Sure."

"Well, a few days after her funeral, I was still pretty out of it. Gillian was crying all the time and Beau was angry. Wouldn't talk to any of us. Just sat in Mom's favorite rocker."

"That skirted one by your dad's bay window? The one upholstered in that funky blue-and-gold fabric that's covered in Revolutionary War flags?"

"That'd be the one. Anyway, after a couple weeks of moping around, one Saturday morning, Dad yanks us out of bed way before dawn, then hauls us to the docks. Back then, Desolation Point didn't have a tourist industry, so we hitched a ride on his buddy Zeke's commercial trawler. Damned thing belched oil and diesel. Stank so bad you wanted to die. Ten minutes in, I was tossing my cookies. Caleb, too. But Gillian and Beau—they came alive out there. The sea did something to them. They caught fish after fish. I don't even remember what kind. For each one they caught, Cap'n Zeke would throw 'em a couple bucks. Me and Caleb were jealous as hell." He shook his head, grinning. "Something about that trip. I don't know. Just made everything better. It didn't bring Mom back, but it made us see life had to go on. That it could even be fun to go on."

"So you got seasick even back then?" she asked, stroking the hair back from his forehead.

"Yep. On land, I can eat anything from week-old pork chops to sour milk, but put me on a boat and I'm a goner."

"So even though you knew this about yourself, you planned this fishing date anyway? Just for me? Because I was being a big baby over my lot in life?"

"You weren't being a baby," he said, taking her hand in his, bringing it to his mouth for a soft kiss. "You *want* a baby. Everyone has their crosses to bear. Hell, some chicks I know get bent out of shape over a zit or mole, but when your brother died, you lost a part of yourself. When you tried taking Craig's place for your dad, you lost a little more of yourself. And so now, here you are in a job you're damned good at, but might not have gone into if it weren't for your father, and it's hit you that the real Charity is ready to come out and play. And, honey, as powerful as you felt using every ounce of your strength wrangling in that fish, you've got to do the same in going after your dream of having a baby."

She nearly swooned. "Anyone ever told you you're adorable?"

LATE MONDAY AFTERNOON at Steph's house, daubing her eyes with a tissue, her sister said, "Adam's so going to propose to you. I predict next weekend, but you could have a ring on your finger as early as midweek."

"No way," Charity said. "Yes, his gesture was incredibly romantic and sweet, but it doesn't prove that he loves me."

"Are you kidding? The man made himself sick making you smile. What more proof do you need?"

Charity left her sister's sofa to pace. "I'm still not sure his act proves anything beyond the fact Adam loves me as a friend—which I already knew."

Stephanie rolled her eyes.

"You can roll your eyes all you want, but not a single thing that transpired yesterday was boyfriend/girlfriend-type stuff. If he's on the verge of proposing, seems to me I'd've had some major lip action."

"But the man was green as that monster fish you caught."

"Correction." Charity cleared her throat. "My magnificent Chinook salmon wasn't green, but silvery, with a blackish streak on his spine."

Stephanie returned to her eye-rolling.

AT HIS FAVORITE table at Ziggy's, Adam tried chilling over a beer, watching a Seahawks vs. Miami game, but worry had him on edge. He was meeting Caleb, Beau and Bug for dinner, and all three were more than thirty minutes late.

Quinton Davis, No. 8 on the Service's Top Ten Most Wanted list, was believed to be in the Portland area. Along with his brothers, Bug had been assigned to the team charged with bringing Quinton in.

Office grapevine had it that Bug and Beau had been key players in cuffing the target outside a neighborhood convenience store where he'd bought cigs and beer nuts. He'd been staying with a *friend* named Luis Vuarez—a slimeball wanted for drug trafficking and four counts of armed robbery.

Adam knew his brothers could take care of themselves, but the thought of Bug being out there facing dangerous scum, made him about six kinds of queasy.

Oh, sure, she beat him at target practice, but that didn't mean he wanted her out there in the field, trying out her skills. He'd always supported female marshals. After all, his sister still worked the occasional sting. But Bug wasn't just any woman. She was his.

Not his woman, per se, as in girlfriend. But as his best friend, he didn't want her in harm's way. Counting his mom and Angela, he'd already lost two women he'd deeply cared about. He wasn't sure he could stand losing Charity.

"Hey, big guy," Caleb said, startling Adam from his thoughts, slapping his back. "How were things in court?"

"Dull," Adam said, nodding at his other brother Beau. "Where's Bug?"

"That all you have to say?" Caleb slid into the half-circle booth. "We pulled off a major coup today. I'd think you'd have some congratulating to do."

"Yeah, yeah," Adam said. "You've never needed me to tell you you're awesome. Now, where's Bug? I thought she was riding with you. She didn't get hurt in the sting, did she?"

"I don't think she's gonna make it," Beau said.

"Why?" Adam jiggled his spoon.

Beau shrugged. "Probably has a hot date with Sam. Those two have been pretty close lately. Shared an order of onion rings at lunch."

Adam bent the spoon in two.

"Take it easy on my silverware," Ziggy said, order pad in hand. The guy was shaped like one of his hamburgers with a shock of self-dyed black hair that looked as if it had been slicked back with a whole can of 10W40.

"Sorry," Adam said, straightening the mangled utensil.

While Caleb and Beau gave Ziggy their orders, Adam couldn't get his mind off Bug standing him up for Suck-up Sam. Couldn't she have at least called to let him know she wasn't coming? And what was the deal with her sharing rings with the guy? Such an intimate act was best shared with friends.

Adam gave Ziggy his order, then settled in to endure a couple hours of comparing diapers and cute-kid stories.

"What's Cal Jr. got planned for the science fair?" Beau asked Caleb.

"He flip-flops between building a volcano and something electronic."

"What kind of electronics?" Beau asked, helping himself to Adam's chips and salsa.

"Guys," Adam complained, "could we please get back to Bug. Is she okay?"

"Why wouldn't she be?" Caleb asked.

"I heard shots were fired. She might've been grazed or something, and you guys just aren't telling me."

Beau sighed. Shook his head. "Give it a rest, man.

She's fine. Probably right now, cuddled with Sam in front of his new flat-screen."

Caleb whistled. "I helped Sam set up his sound system, and let me tell you, that baby rocks. Bug'll love it. Oh—and this was cute. Bear said Sam was laying in a huge supply of those cookies she likes, just so—"

"Fudge grahams?" Adam interjected.

"How'd you know?"

Adam shrugged. "Lucky guess."

Beau and Caleb ignored him, rambling on about Suck-up Sam and his lame TV. Bug wasn't really falling for the guy just because of his impressive gadgets, was she? In a potential husband, she should be studying deeper issues. Trustworthiness and loyalty. He'd have to be a good provider and dad. A good listener and friend.

Like himself.

Not that he was putting himself up for the job. But if he had been, he'd be perfect. Maybe if he'd met Bug before Angela, things might've turned out differently, but it was a little late in the game for second-guessing. What was done was done, and Bug deserved better than a busted-up head case like himself.

"Adam?" Caleb asked.

"Huh?" He looked up.

"You seen Sam's movie collection? When you get a chance, you should check it out. Bug said it was mighty impressive."

Adam growled.

"WHERE HAVE YOU been?" Adam asked from a bench outside Bug's building. It was past nine, and cold enough for him to see his breath.

"Excuse me?" she asked, her sexy pear scent reaching him before she did. What was she thinking wearing that stuff around Sam?

"Our date? Ziggy's? Ring any bells? Or were you too busy fawning over Sam's TV you forgot your friends?"

She wrinkled her nose. "Are your allergies bothering you, and you accidentally overdosed?"

"What's that supposed to mean?" he asked, pushing to his feet, falling into step beside her.

Mounting the building's stairs, she shot him an odd, sad sort-of look. Was she worried about him? "You seem...*off.*"

"I'm good," he said, getting the door for her. "It's you I'm worried about. Spending so much time with Sam. It's going to louse up any progress you might make in finding a real father for your baby."

"Stop," she said, ducking under his outstretched arm on her way inside.

"What am I doing?"

"Acting like a jealous lover. And for your information, I wasn't with Sam tonight, but Steph."

"Oh." Waiting with her for the next available of the building's three elevators, he shoved his hands into his pockets. "For your information," he said after they'd waited a good two or three minutes. "I wasn't acting like a jealous *lover,* but a concerned friend."

Old Mrs. Kleypus wandered up with her Pekingese, Gringo, and judging by her gaping mouth, apparently just in time to catch Adam's speech.

"Charity, dear," she said while Gringo lifted his leg on the plastic ivy flanking the left side of the elevator door. "Is this foul-mouthed hooligan bothering you? If he is, Clive is just down the hall. I'll be happy to get him."

Now there was a frightening prospect. Adam worked hard to hide a chuckle. Clive was Washington Manor's security guard and, judging by the last time prankster teens had gotten away with dressing the building's George Washington garden statue in drag, Gringo the Peeing Wonder Dog would've had better odds of drowning visitors up to no good.

Mrs. Kleypus knew full well Charity was a gun-toting marshal, quite capable of taking care of herself. Still, the ornery old woman persisted in giving Adam grief every time he came around.

"No, ma'am," Charity said, flashing the nosy old bat a much sweeter smile than she'd given him all day. "Thanks so much for asking, but I think I can handle this on my own. No need to interrupt Clive's shows."

"All right, then," Mrs. Kleypus said, scratching her hip with one hand, yanking Gringo's pink leash with her other. "But call if you need me. I'll be in all evening."

"I will," Charity said just as the elevator announced its arrival with a loud ding. "Thanks again for your help."

"You're welcome, dear."

Adam hustled Bug onto the elevator, punching the close-door button five times in rapid succession.

In Bug's unit, he made a beeline to the fridge for beer and cold mac and cheese, then parked on the sofa, using the remote to flick on the TV.

"Make yourself at home," Bug said.

"Did you want a beer?" he asked while she stood staring at him from behind the coffee table. "Here, take this one. I'll get another."

She sighed. "It's not beer I want, Adam, but an explanation for why you've been acting so bizarre."

"Don't have a clue what you mean," he said, turning up "Trading Spaces" on the Learning Channel.

"Case in point," she said, storming over to the TV and shutting it off. "You despise this show. Every time it's on, you say—and I quote, 'I could make a house look a damn sight better with a thousand bucks. Just arm me with a can of paint and a new TV.'"

"I never say that." Gazing out the window over the kitchen sink, jiggling his right foot, he added, "And if anyone has been acting bizarre, it's you."

"How?"

"You want specifics?"

"If it's not too much trouble."

"All right. For starters, how about the fact that

this is like the third time you've stood me up for a dinner date."

"Correct me if I'm wrong," she said, "but wasn't it you who said we don't have dates, but *meetings?*"

He scratched his head.

"Well?"

"You know what I mean. If you had a meeting with Franks, would you just not show up without even the benefit of a courtesy call? I know you've got a cell phone. Did you forget how to use it?"

"That's it." Her eyes got all big and wet and she pointed to the door. "I've tried being nice to you. I tried helping with your stupid scheme to dupe your shrink. I was even dumb enough to think whatever it is we share might actually be going somewhere, but you're hopeless. No woman will ever catch you."

"Duh," he said. "Because I was already caught by Angela Jacobs."

"She's dead, Adam. What don't you get about that fact?"

Chapter Seven

"What are you saying?" Adam demanded.

Bug threw her hands in the air, dropping them with a dramatic smack against her thighs. "I give up," she muttered on her way to the bedroom.

"No," he said, springing off the sofa. "You're not going to throw something like that on the table, then just walk away. Finish what you started."

She slammed the bedroom door.

He barreled down the hall, jerking open the door. "Why are you so jealous of what I shared with Angela? God knows you bring her up enough."

"And you don't?" Bug asked. She stood at her bedroom window, arms crossed, expression thunderous and impossible to read.

"I almost married Angela," he said. "Doesn't that give me a right to talk about her?"

"Of course," she said with a half laugh. "Forgive me for being so obtuse."

"No, really. You started this. Tell me why it makes

you so crazy whenever I so much as mention Angela's name? If I didn't know better, I'd say you were trying to replace the part she played in my life."

"You dare ask me that after lecturing me on how no one can replace a dead loved one?" She shook her head. "Yes, I was a kid and did the only thing I knew how to do to help my dad through an awful time. And yes, as an adult, I'm still playing catch-up to find the real me, but you, Adam Logue, are a complete whack job. Do you even admit to yourself you have serious issues when it comes to letting go of the past? The last thing I want to do is replace Angela, or the special place she warms in your heart. But it might be nice for you to make a little new room in there—if not for me, then at least yourself. I, at least, realize I have no life, and am trying to change it. You, on the other hand, think everything's just hunky-dory."

He stood there staring, wanting to say something, but he was unsure where to begin.

"Go home, Adam." She wrapped her arms even tighter around herself. "You're no longer welcome here."

He snorted. "That's a helluva thing to say to your best friend."

"*Ex*-best friend."

Shaking his head, Adam abided by her wishes.

WHEN ADAM CLOSED her condo door, Charity gave in to the slow tremble that'd been building ever since encountering him on that bench outside her building. Dammit. He had to feel something more than friendship for her. *Had* to. Steph thought so, too. Every bone in Charity's body told her Adam was hiding from his own feelings, but knowing that did nothing to help her work through her own.

Loving Adam was akin to loving a rock.

No, she thought, crossing to the bed, flopping onto the pile of pillows at the head. That wasn't fair. In his own way, Adam was incredibly sweet. This weekend's fishing trip, for instance. He'd put an incalculable amount of heart and thought into the outing, but to what end? To help her overcome her issues over her lack of confidence, so she might ultimately land a man other than himself?

Right. Seeing how he'd reacted this afternoon on the mere suspicion she'd been with Sam, she didn't believe for one second Adam wanted to see her with anyone but him. But even knowing that, what could she do?

Her sister had come up with a myriad of supposedly perfect plans for luring him into her feminine spell. And they'd worked, but unless Adam gave up Angela's ghost, she might as well forget the whole thing. They'd be great friends forever—of that, she was certain—but friendship wouldn't give her a baby to cuddle and rock. Friendship wouldn't give her a loving partner to share her child's firsts with. Kindergarten parent/teacher conferences and attending Disney movies on premiere weekends. Building snowmen and making Fourth of July ice cream. Sure, all of it sounded corny and sappy sweet, but she wanted it all. Her whole life, she'd fought to succeed in a man's world, and now she wanted to conquer womanhood—in every sense of the word.

Was she a head case for dreaming of such wonders? And what about her job? Yes, it was deep within a man's world, but it'd become her world, too. She'd made great friends, and each time she poured every ounce of her soul and sweat into taking down a bad guy, it felt so damned good. So how was she supposed to do all of that, and still have time to be a great mom? Yes, Gillian had managed to snag the best of both worlds, but Charity had to wonder if she was just fooling herself into believing she could have it all, too.

Funny, though, how even knowing the absurdity of her quest did nothing to diminish the wanting.

And so she cried herself to sleep, waking with quiet determination to finally, ultimately, make a clean break from Adam. She'd begun the process before, but until now, hadn't taken the vow seriously.

She wasn't sure how, but some way—today—she would free her heart from its futile quest for Adam Logue's love.

"EXCUSE ME, SIR?" Charity said to her boss, Franks, Friday morning. "Might I have a moment of your time?"

"Caldwell," he said with a grunt. "Good work you did helping to capture No. 8. I was just coming to find you."

"Oh?" His office was plush, and her black pumps made no sound on the thick beige carpet.

"Sit."

"Yessir." She planted herself in one of the supple navy-leather guest chairs facing his desk.

"What's on your mind?"

"Actually, sir, I was coming to request a transfer—"

A knock sounded on the office door, then Beau, Caleb, Bear, Sam and a sullen, red-eyed Adam strolled through.

"Great," Franks said. "All of you have a seat. Something's come up that I'd like you to handle."

"Sir," Charity said. "I really—"

"After this assignment, Caldwell, we'll talk, but until then, I need your attention one-hundred-percent focused on the task at hand. Understood?"

"Yessir," she said, Adam's presence causing goose bumps to rise on her forearms. Hopefully, this assignment would just be a short-lived thing, like the one she'd just finished with his brothers.

"Here's the deal," Franks said, standing, then plucking a thick pile of folders from his desk before passing them to the marshals. "For the foreseeable future, you will be handling a high-profile security case. Federal Judge Norton in Cedarville has received numerous death threats in conjunction with the trial he's presiding over."

From the sofa, Caleb whistled, his nose buried in his copy of the files. "This brings back nasty memories."

"I'll bet," Franks said. "Sorry about that, but as one of my best men, I need you heading this team."

"Absolutely," Caleb said.

Best as Charity could remember, Caleb's wife, Allie, had been threatened by a particularly bloodthirsty white supremacist group.

Charity closed her eyes for a split second. She felt for this Judge Norton. Truly, she did. But she was on the verge of a major panic attack just being in the same room with Adam, and now she was supposed to be cooped up with him in the close quarters and endless hours high-profile security teams faced?

She opened her eyes to find Adam staring at her and sharply looked away.

"Caleb," Franks said, "I'll leave it to your discretion to make individual duty assignments. For now, all of you have exactly one hour to gather gear, make goodbyes to loved ones, and meet back here, ready to roll. Questions?"

When no one raised a hand, Franks dismissed them.

On the way out, Adam followed her into the hall. Unfortunately, because she'd been first into Franks's office, she was last out, making her an easy target.

"We need to talk," he said, fingers encircling her upper arm.

"Adam, not now. I've got a lot to do in the next hour."

"Duh. I just want you to know that I plan to handle this assignment in a professional manner. Whatever's bugging you, I respectfully ask you to leave it here. We'll pick it up when we get home."

Staring at him incredulously, she shook her head and laughed. "Do you hear what you're saying?" she said, wrenching her arm free, pointing her index finger at his chest. "I'm not the one making a big deal out of the way things were left last night. You are."

Sharply exhaling, he said, "I should've known you'd make this hard."

"Again, Adam, all I'm doing is trying to get home to pack a few clothes. Now, would you mind letting me pass, or are you planning to tag along and deck yourself out in my jeans and T-shirts?"

He shot her a look of utter disgust and stormed off toward his cubicle.

She snatched her purse, then high-tailed it home for her last private breakdown before what was by no intention of her own about to become a very public relationship disaster.

EARLY FRIDAY EVENING, on the shore of a fir-lined, glassy lake far too idyllic for gunplay, Adam and the rest of the team stood outside Judge Norton's fishing cabin—where he'd chosen to stay until his court-room could be repaired following a fire set by the defendant's pregnant wife, now in custody. From the file he'd read on the endless ride up, Adam learned local marshals had thought her incarceration would be the end of the judge's threats, but the threats persisted, worsening in severity.

"All right," Caleb said to his five-man, one-woman team. "Sam, Bear, I want you two covering the first shift. Beau and I will back you up. Charity, Adam, you head to the judge's guest cabin, which will be our base of operations. I want you two rested up for—"

"But, Caleb," Adam interjected, swatting at a pesky fly. "I'd feel more comfortable—"

"Can it," Caleb said. "Charity has the best night vision of any of us. You've got second best. Making you two my late-night team."

"But—"

"Got a problem, little bro, take it up with Franks."

Oh, did Adam have problems. So many, he couldn't begin to count. Lucky for him, he wouldn't have had time even if he'd wanted to as Caleb gestured him and Bug to be on their way to the team's temporary office.

"TOP OR BOTTOM?" Adam asked, pointing to the single-room cabin's bunk bed. When Bug kept her lips clamped shut, he repeated the question, then asked, "What do you want?"

She shrugged. "I guess, top."

"I thought you liked bottom?"

"Last time we got stuck with bunk beds," she said, hefting her sole bag onto a chair she'd pushed alongside the bed, "I was on bottom, and the top bunk kept creaking. That whole three weeks I had visions of the thing falling, flattening me like a pancake."

"Why didn't you say something?" Adam asked, kicking off his shoes, then settling into his bunk. "I'd've traded."

Charity kept silent as she plucked off her black heels and suit coat. The short skirt had ridden up her thighs, and her light green blouse looked badly rumpled. Adam wished her windblown hair and weary expression turned him off, but if anything, it made Charity appear vulnerable. Making him want to tug her down onto his bunk and into his arms.

Of course, she was a far cry from vulnerable. As his brother had already pointed out, she boasted the best marksmanship scores of any of them. But knowing that didn't stop his wanting. It didn't fill the empty place in the pit of his stomach that'd been there ever since she'd booted him out of her home for the second time.

"You're not planning on working this security detail in those kind of get-ups, are you?" he blurted. Because if she was, he wasn't sure how he was supposed to think of her strictly as a fellow agent and not as the woman he'd come damned close to sleeping with.

"Get a brain," she said sarcastically. She unzipped her suitcase, pulling out black jeans and a black sweatshirt. "I wouldn't even be wearing it now if Franks had given us enough time. I barely had time to pack." She stood there with her clothes in her arms. "Do you mind?"

"What?"

"Looking away while I change?"

"It's not like I haven't seen it all before. Especially since you've been sleeping in that hot little Victoria's Secret get-up."

"Nice," she said, lips pursed, padding off to the utilitarian bathroom, slamming the door.

Hand to his forehead, Adam sighed.

It was going to be a long night.

AFTER CHANGING, Charity sat on the closed toilet seat, cradling her forehead in her hands. If she survived this assignment, however long it lasted, it'd be a miracle.

"Bug?" Adam knocked on the bathroom door. "Can I come in?"

"No. Just a minute, and it'll be your turn."

"I don't have to go," he said. "I want to talk."

Her eyebrows shot up. In the history of the world, had any man ever made such an outrageous statement?

The bathroom was so small that from her seat all she had to do was lean forward to open the door. "What?"

"I'm sorry," he said.

"No, I am. I've been too sensitive lately about a lot of things."

"Because of your womanly transformation?" he asked, catching her in the act of smoothing her hair.

"No. I'm over that." She made a face. "Not that I'm well and truly over it, but you know what I mean. I've got bigger issues."

"Like wanting to have kids."

"That's one of them."

"What else?"

She sighed. "Can we just call a truce and leave it at that?"

"Sam being an ass? 'Cause if he isn't treating you right, just say the word and I'll—"

Shaking her head, shooting Adam her most disgusted look, Charity stood, brushing by him on her way back to the cabin's main room.

He followed. "That's it, isn't it? He didn't physically hurt you, did he? Or is he messing with your mind? Either way, I'll—"

"Quit it!" she shrieked. "For the last time, Sam and I *aren't* an item. I don't know who keeps putting that in your head."

"You don't have to lie," he said with a gentle touch of her shoulder. "Domestic abuse isn't an easy issue, but together, we—"

Hands over his flapping lips, she said, "Seriously, Adam. Sam isn't the problem."

"Then what is it?" How was it when her chest was actually tight with fury for the man, his hot, moist breath made her fingers and stomach tingle?

"You," she blurted. "Okay? If you want the truth, my biggest problem in life is you." There, she'd said it. It was out there for the whole world to hear. Adam *was* her world, only he was too blind to see it. What the two of them might share if he'd only take a few minuscule steps out of his past with a ghost lover for a glimpse into a brighter future with the living, breathing woman standing in front of him.

"Me?" He laughed. *Laughed!* "I'm your biggest problem? That's bogus. How can I be a problem? I'm your best friend."

Turning her back on him, she climbed the short ladder leading to her bunk. "*Ex*-best friend."

"You know, Bug," he said a whole six inches from her head. Did he have to be so tall that her planned escape had only put her in an even more exasperating proximity? "I'm getting sick and tired of you always being grumpy with me when here I've been going out of my way to be nice. Hell, I even bought you a car, yet still, that's not enough."

"I said thank you."

"Doesn't matter. You owe me."

"That's crazy."

"Maybe so, but—"

The cabin's screen door creaked open and Beau

stepped inside. "Would you two knock off the verbal foreplay? We can hear you all the way over at the judge's cabin."

"Yeah, sure," Adam said.

She rolled over and groaned.

"Charity?" Beau asked. "You pack any of those Rice Krispies Treats cookie-bar things?"

"Sorry," she said. "Boss didn't leave much time for baking before we left town."

"S'okay," he said, snatching a minibag of chips from their meager supply box. "Hey, since you two obviously aren't catching any z's, how 'bout heading back to town for grub? Ever since I found out me and Gracie are pregnant, seems like I can't get enough to eat."

Before Charity could turn down his request, Beau was gone, whistling across the sun-flooded yard.

"Thanks," Charity mumbled.

"What'd I do?"

"Nothing," she said, scooting down the bunk to the ladder. *Nothing except make me fall in love with you, then build an insurmountable wall around your heart.*

But was that Adam's problem, or her own? Here she was, furious with him for not loving her, yet she was the one who'd less than twenty-four hours earlier vowed to clinically cut him from her life. With that in mind, was it fair for her to continue the Ms. Freeze routine? The guy was bending over backward to be nice to her.

Besides which, she was on duty, working at a job she loved. When she got back to Portland, there'd be plenty of time to search for the perfect husband and father for her baby. In the meantime, maybe it would be best to bury the hatchet with Adam.

Once she'd landed on her feet, he shocked her by pulling her into his arms, planting silly little kisses along her cheek and ear. "What do I have to do to be back on your official friends list?"

"You're on," she said, scrunching her neck, half-heartedly trying to back away, wholeheartedly savoring his every touch.

"Partially on?" he teased, his latest peck landing perilously close to her lips. "Or all the way on. Like things will finally go back to normal?"

"Depends on your definition of normal," she said, her concentration waning. When one of his kisses did land on her lips, she couldn't be sure of anything.

Except Adam.

He deepened the kiss, taking the mood from playful to hot in under sixty seconds. "Mmm…" he moaned. "We shouldn't be doing this."

"I know," she said, sliding her fingers into his hair.

"We're almost, sort of, on duty."

"Uh-huh…"

He slipped his hands into the back pockets of her jeans, giving her a squeeze. "That kiss wasn't normal."

"Excuse me?"

He removed his hands from her pockets and skimmed them over her hips, settling them at her waist. "We don't normally kiss like that."

"Seems to me," she said, clearing her throat, "we don't normally kiss at all."

"True."

"So what's that say about our friendship?" With her forehead resting against his chest, feeling his pounding heart, she was almost afraid to ask, "This mean it's shot to hell?"

"Can't be," he said, hands now on her cheeks, thumbs tracing her eyebrows. "Because if that were true, I wouldn't still have this craving to be around you every second of every day."

"Adam…" *If that's true, don't you see what that means? That what we share goes way deeper than friendship? That whether you want to admit it or not, we're in love?*

"We'd better get those groceries," he said. "Or Beau's going to have our asses."

Is that it? Is that really all you have to say?

"Ready?" he asked.

Swallowing a hard knot of tears, she nodded. "Let me grab my shoes."

Chapter Eight

"Wanna just get a bunch of frozen food?" Adam asked at the grocery store, trying his damnedest to keep the subject on food and off the unfamiliar, unpleasant tangle of emotions wadded in his chest. What was the deal with Bug? He didn't used to feel so antsy around her—as if she were a real girl. She used to just be another one of the guys, only more fun to hang out with because she…

What? What specifically was it about her that made him crave being with her more than, say, Bear?

"Fun idea," she said. "But seeing how the cabin only has a small fridge, we might want to stick to basics. Hot dogs and mac and cheese."

"Good call," he said, struggling not to notice her scent as she ducked under his outstretched arm to grab a few cans of SpaghettiOs. Was she still using that pear stuff? He'd like to see her back in that negligee. She could call it a nightgown, but he didn't just stumble out of the turnip patch. He'd been around the block enough times to know what women slept in versus what they *played* in.

"Beanie Weenies?" she asked on the next aisle, holding out two cans.

"Huh?"

"What's the matter with you?" she asked. "Considering that we'll be stuck out at that cabin for at least the next two days, we're making vital decisions here."

"True."

"So what's it going to be?" She was back to waving the cans.

He slipped his hands around her waist, pulling her in for another kiss—the only thing he currently had a taste for.

"Adam," she said with a giggle, glancing over her shoulder at a nosy old guy staring with rapt interest. "What's gotten into you?"

"Honestly," he said. "I'm not sure. "Kissing you all of a sudden seems more fun than chips or cookies or X-Box or even watching football."

"And this is a bad thing?" she asked, eyebrows raised.

"It is considering the fact that I'm incapable of offering you anything deeper than friendship."

"What if that turned out to not be true?"

Pushing the cart away from her, he said, "I'm not following."

"Yes, you are, or you wouldn't be walking away."

"Correction—I'm shopping."

"You're avoiding the question." As much as Adam hated to admit it, she was right. And that thought didn't help his hot flash, already in progress. Should he turn the cart around and try shoving himself into one of the stand-up freezers? "You haven't been talking to my shrink, have you?"

"No," she said, hands on her hips. "And now that you mention it, what happens with your therapy, seeing how you'll be on this assignment for the unforeseeable future?"

He shrugged around the end of the cereal aisle. "I'm thinking I'm pretty much cured."

Bug snorted.

A white-haired sample lady was passing out coupons for fiber tablets. They both passed.

"What's that mean?" Adam asked once they were on their own with nothing but some Sousa march blaring from hidden overhead speakers.

"It means, you've got more issues than an entire season of *The O.C.*"

BACK AT THE CABIN, Charity helped Adam unload the food, then, while Adam grabbed a quick shower and nap, she trekked outside for a briefing on how the afternoon had gone for their partners. She assumed all was quiet, but with close-mouthed Beau and Caleb, you never knew.

"Caleb?" she called when she'd walked the perimeter of the judge's cabin and found nothing but a yard in major need of mowing. "Beau? Sam? Bear?"

Nothing.

Assuming for whatever odd reason, they must all be inside, Charity rapped on the cabin's front door, but got no answer. Pulse pounding, she took the liberty of trying the door. It was open, and she crept inside. "Judge Norton? Caleb?"

The cabin was larger than the one she and Adam had spent the past couple hours stocking, and the furnishings were much more posh, with rich-smelling leather sofas and chairs and rows of leather-bound books. There were top-of-the-line appliances in the kitchen and black granite counters. The place didn't smell musty like their cabin, either. More like fruity potpourri.

"Hello?" she called again. "Anyone home?"

She checked the bathroom, but when that yielded no results, she ran back to her own cabin for Adam.

"Wake up," she said, giving him a shake.

"Huh? What's wrong?"

"Not sure. Judge Norton and the rest of our crew are gone. I've tried each team member's cell and radio with no answers from any of them."

"Caleb's SUV still outside?" he asked, sitting up, narrowly avoiding hitting his head on the low bunk above him.

"Yes."

"Well, then, they can't have gone far." He'd taken

off his sweatshirt, and Charity had to force herself to look away while he tugged it back on. Good grief, what was wrong with her? They were here on official business—not funny business. This was not an appropriate time to be eyeing his buff pecs and abs. "Come on," he said, hopping on one foot while slipping on his tennis shoe. "Let me grab my piece and radio, and we'll split up to check out the lakeside trails."

When an hour's search netted nothing, Charity was genuinely worried. There was no sign of struggle, but then if plans had changed to the extent that Caleb had packed up the judge and taken off in another marshal's vehicle, wouldn't he have at least had the professionalism to leave a note?

"Any sign of them?" Adam's voice came over her handheld radio.

"Nothing," she replied.

"Now what?" He crunched around the bend in the trail not twenty feet from the lakeside tumble of rocks where she stood.

Grinning at his antics of still using his radio even though she was in sight, she shrugged, clipping her radio back on to her belt. "This whole thing has been voodoo from the start. Just hasn't felt right."

"How so?" he asked, backing onto the root of a massive fallen fir. A light breeze rippled the lake and shushed through the evergreens, but a pair of Canada geese floating along didn't seem to mind the sudden chill. Charity watched as a Japanese beetle, *Popillia japonica* made its way across the dirt path.

"Think about it. Protecting this judge was supposed to be high profile, yet here we sit, out of radio contact with the rest of the team. Procedure for any protective mission, no matter how small, clearly states all team members must be in radio contact at all times."

"Maybe the rest of the guys forgot?"

"Bear, maybe. Caleb, Beau and Sam?" She laughed, darting out of range of a bumblebee wanting to land on her ear.

"Yeah, guess you're right. So? What now?"

She sighed, gazing at the glassy lake while keeping a wary eye on that bee. "Report in to Franks, see if he's heard anything. Then sit back and wait."

"Well?" Charity asked five minutes later when Adam pressed the off button on his cell. "What'd Franks say?"

"You're not gonna believe this, but Franks wasn't there, so I talked to his secretary."

"And…"

"She said Caleb's radio was down so he couldn't contact us directly, but that we're to meet him at some drive-in theater about twenty miles north. Seems the judge got a hankering for civilization."

"What?" Plunking onto the tree trunk beside him, she scratched her head. "Supposing that's true, did Caleb lose your cell number? And mine? And what happened to the rest of the guys' radios? Surely all four didn't go bad at the same time? And how did they get to civilization, seeing how Caleb's SUV is still here?"

Adam shrugged.

"Voodoo," she said, pushing herself up. "I don't like this one bit. What if whoever's trying to get to the judge somehow rerouted our radio signals to—"

"Get a grip." Adam kicked a dirt clod. "And then what? You think this assassin also paid off Mrs. Swenson, who's been an official U.S. Marshal's secretary for about the last eighty years, to give us false information?"

"You sure it was her?" Charity asked, falling into step with him as they headed down the dried mud trail leading back to the cabins.

"Reasonably, sure. I guess it could've been an imposter, but what are the odds?"

"Guess you're right. So now what?"

"We pack a few firearms, Twinkies and chips, then head for the drive-in."

ADAM THUMPED the heel of his hand against the company SUV's hood. "This is really starting to piss me off. So if they're not here, and none of them is answering the phone, then—"

Bug's cell rang.

She glanced at the Caller ID. "It's Caleb," she said to Adam before answering. "Where are you?"

She fell silent for a few seconds. "Uh-huh… But… Okay. See you then. Oh—one more thing. I've got a guy asking what color my new car is. How exactly would you describe that shade?…Will do. Thanks."

"Well?" Adam asked. During the call, he'd done his best to eavesdrop, but a long-haired doper in a Trans-Am pulled into the space beside them with old school Aerosmith blaring. Two Miller Lite cans clattered out the open door when he reached for his speaker. The car's exhaust still hung in the air, making Adam even grumpier than he'd been before.

"Your brother apologized for losing contact with us. Said their cells must've been out of range."

Adam snorted. "But not ours?"

"Wait—it gets better. Their radio batteries were dead."

"Right." Lips set in a grim line, Adam asked, "Where are they now?"

"Back at the cabin. The judge got tired and decided he didn't want to stay for the movie, after all. But Caleb told me to tell you that we should go ahead and stay. They've got everything under control."

"And Caleb answered your car color question okay? It didn't sound like he was under duress?" he asked, referring to the prearranged code they'd use to signify trouble.

She wrinkled her nose at the cigarette smoke billowing from the Trans-Am's open windows. "He even went so far as to praise me for using the code."

Adam whistled. "You were right. This is pure voodoo."

"What do you want to do?" she asked, climbing back into the SUV's passenger side.

"Obviously we can't stay for the movie. We've got to go check out Caleb's story."

"Granted."

"So let's head back to the cabin. After that, we'll reassess."

"CHARITY? What are you doing here?" Caleb asked at the front door of the judge's cabin. He checked his watch. "The movie was a double feature. You're not supposed to be back for another four or five hours."

She tried edging past him, but he veered to his right, blocking her view of the poker tourney being held at the kitchen table.

"What's going on?" she whispered, her shadowed features clearly worried. "You in trouble?"

Caleb had to chuckle to himself. He wasn't in trouble now, but would be if this mission didn't end as planned. It'd taken some doing to arrange for everyone involved in this romance heist to have vacation time, but hopefully, the end result would be worth their efforts. "I'm good," he said. "Why?"

"Level with me." She tucked her hands into her jean pockets. "Adam and I aren't dumb. We know something's not right. Want us to call for reinforcements?"

"Totally unnecessary," he said, edging out of the

cabin, then tugging the heavy wood door firmly shut behind him. "Where's my brother?"

"Bathroom. He'll be here shortly."

"Good, good. I need to brief you two on the night's duties."

Nodding, she said, "It's about time we accomplished something. I was beginning to feel like a fifth wheel."

"No need for that," he said, slapping her back. "Trust me, you are vital to the success of this assignment."

Adam wandered up, then, after a few more minutes of small talk, Caleb said, "Now, here's what I want you to do…."

"HAVE I MENTIONED lately how *off* this whole case is?" Charity asked, resting her socks-clad feet on the dash. It was three-fifteen in the morning, and so far, the only thing they'd seen on their stakeout of the dirt road leading to the cabins was a waddling opossum family and two small deer.

"Yeah, well, at least we're finally doing something constructive."

"What's constructive about this?"

"Unless our bad guys are 'coptering in, we'll be the one's taking them down."

"Oh, boy," she said with the latest of what was starting to be a long string of sighs. "Sounds fun."

"Damned straight." He shot her a devilish grin she tried to ignore, but dammit, there it was, that little tingle in the pit of her stomach. "And since when do you not enjoy taking out a few well-deserving thugs?"

"I don't know," she said, taking her feet down to sit cross-legged on the big bucket seat. "Guess since getting the mommy itch, I've lost my gung-ho edge. Don't get me wrong. I still get a hankering for a good adrenaline rush every now and then, but I'm just as happy adding a new bug to my collection as I used to be firing off rounds."

She wasn't ready to quit her job, but when she did find the right guy who wanted to have that baby as badly as her, she'd certainly be willing to pare down to a part-time schedule. She'd never been one to take unnecessary chances in her job, and once she was a mom, it would be doubly important to play it safe. Not only that, but why have a baby if she couldn't spend time with him or her, sharing all those special firsts?

Listen to her. *The right guy. That baby.* All of her hopes and dreams for the future were hopelessly vague. And for what? All because Adam didn't have the romance-sense God had given a tree stump.

"That it?" he asked, helping himself to her last can of diet root beer.

"What else would there be?"

He took her last Oreo, too. Finished chewing, ignoring her put-out look, he said, "Now that you're going to be a mom, I figure you worry about if something happened to you, what would happen to the baby."

"I'm not pregnant yet."

"No, but you will be. You're gorgeous, smart, funny. Make damned good queso. What guy wouldn't want you to have his kid?"

The question brought instant tears stinging to her eyes. Maybe because she was dead tired, or maybe just temporarily insane, she couldn't keep from asking, "If I'm so great, how come you wouldn't want me to have your baby?"

"W-what?" He choked on his latest sip of her soda. "Where'd that come from?"

"Never mind," she said with a wistful smile, not surprised by his reaction, just saddened. But then, what had she expected? For him to leap from his seat and propose?

He angled toward her, messing with strands of her newly cropped hair. "Moonlight suits you."

"What's that supposed to mean?"

He shrugged.

She looked down, took a deep breath. "That question—about why you wouldn't want me pregnant with your child—it was a joke."

"Sure," he said. "I know."

"Good, because I wouldn't want you to think—"

"But what if it hadn't been?"

Heart thundering, palms sweating, she peered past her reflection in the window to the shadowy forest. By day, it was a beautiful place. By night, it was spooky and tangled and scary. Kind of like the way she felt about Adam when he posed hypothetical questions.

"Charity? What if I said I want to help you have a baby?"

"You called me by name."

"Yeah? So? Bug is my friend and partner. This goes deeper than either of those relationships."

"You're serious? You'd want to go through the whole sperm-donor routine?"

He cringed. "Whatever happened to making babies the old-fashioned way?"

"Then you'd want to…"

"Hell, yeah," he said with a sizzling grin that made his offer awfully hard to resist.

"Nice as that sounds," she said, flashing a shy smile of her own, "I—"

"Nice?" From low in his throat came a growling sound, then, cupping his hand to the back of her head, he pulled her in for a hungry kiss. "Darlin', the things I could show you would be miles from nice. More like bad—in a really great way."

"Whew," she said, fanning cheeks she hoped it was too dark for him to see blushing. "Was that a baby-making audition?"

"Want it to be?"

"What if I said yes?"

"Then I'd say, let's get busy. With any luck, we'll have a baby on the way within an hour."

"That sure of yourself?" she said with a smirk.

He took both her hands in his and squeezed. "That sure of *us*. We're gonna make gorgeous babies."

The tears were back. In a million years, she couldn't have thought of a more perfect thing for him to say at a more perfect time.

Not thinking, just doing, just being beyond-belief happy, she tossed her arms around his neck for a hug, kissing his cheeks, chin and forehead. "Yes, yes, yes. I love you, Adam Logue. I've loved you for years. I was beginning to fear this day might never come, but finally, you asked me to marry you." Pulling back, wanting to trace the features of his dear face that would soon be duplicated on a whole brood of children, she asked, "Who should we tell first?"

Even in shadow-tinted moonlight, she could tell he looked confused. "Whoa. Back up. I love you, too, gorgeous, but somewhere along the line, I think we crossed wires. I asked you to make love—and a baby—not to get hitched. I already told you, what happened with Angela showed me a lot. I let her down, her parents, the Marshals Service. You deserve a great life, Charity, starting with a guy a helluva lot better than me."

"That's a cop-out."

"What?" Even in the shadowy light, she could see his expression was one of quiet fury.

"I think your problem is that losing Angela hurt. Not just your heart, but pride. I think you just don't want to put yourself through that again."

"Hell, yes, I'm hurt. Who wouldn't be? She died in my arms. Do you have any idea what that was like?"

"Yes, as a matter of fact I do. Convenient how you forget other people have painful pasts, too, Adam. I might've just been a kid, but standing in that sterile hospital room, watching my brother drag his last breaths, watching my mother shriek and shake and completely fall apart, watching my dad just stand there, telling Craig to 'Hold on, son, you'll be fine'—you think that was fun?"

"You're twisting my words."

And you're twisting my heart!

Adam had no idea how much he was hurting her right now. The pain in her chest was both crushing and sharp. How could she have been so stupid as to just blurt out all of that? About how much she loved him, and how she'd been waiting for him to return that love for so long. Of course, he hadn't been asking her to marry him. How could she have been such a dolt?

He was back to holding her hands, but she pushed him away, shoved her feet into her lightweight hiking boots, then opened her door and jumped into the cold, damp night.

Adam didn't want her. Just a quick roll on the bottom bunk.

Fool me once, shame on you.

Fool me twice, shame on me.

Only what Charity currently felt wasn't so much shame, as fury.

Chapter Nine

"Bug—Charity—wait!" Adam shouted after her. But Charity slammed the SUV door on him and his words. Running, running until there were footsteps chasing her and Adam was pulling her to a stop, dragging her sobbing into his arms.

It was mortifying for him to see her like this. Vulnerable. Emotionally naked. She had no more secrets. Her every card lay on the table.

"I'm an ass," he said into her hair, his words spilling in a warm cloud she wanted to wrap herself in, blocking out the cold reality of loving him. "Yes, we've both been dealt crappy blows. And you have to believe I truly love you. I just—"

"No," she said, sniffling, wiping her runny nose. "I went into this with my eyes open. You've never been anything but honest with me where Angela's concerned."

At that moment Adam might as well have been shot just as his first love had been, for surely a bullet couldn't hurt as bad as seeing this woman he loved sobbing her heart out. He did love Charity.

But because of Angela's death, he was forever cursed. There was a black mark on his soul. If he'd never fallen so hard for her, maybe his life would've turned out differently. Maybe he'd be with her now.

Only the really sick thing was, he didn't want to be with Angela—he wanted to be with Charity. To hold her like this forever. Kiss her till she quit crying, then make love to her until dawn. He wanted to go out and buy her the biggest, gaudiest engagement ring his meager savings could afford, then marry her in a giant wedding with all of their friends and family standing by. After that, he'd take her on a honeymoon and start on that baby she wanted. And he'd be a dad. A damned good dad. A damned good husband and provider. Working night and day if that's what it took to make his little family comfortable and happy and— He abruptly released Bug to scrub his face with his hands.

What was he doing?

Blaspheming Angela's memory this way. She'd loved him and trusted him and he'd let her down. And right now, in wanting to be with another woman, he was doing it again. More unforgivable was the chance that if he gave in to this insanity, he'd only end up letting Charity down, as well.

Yeah, his conscience interjected, but his brother-in-law, Joe, had been married before Gillian. Adam had never viewed him as any lesser man because of having found a second shot at love. But Joe's first wife's death hadn't been his fault. He hadn't been there, holding her in his arms when she'd died, thinking that if only he'd turned six inches to his right, the assassin's bullet would've hit him.

"What're you thinking?" Bug asked.

"Long story."

"I am sorry about blurting all that, Adam. I never meant to put you on the spot."

"I know." He pulled her deeper into his arms. "And I never should've said all that about us having a kid. I mean, yeah, sure, we could go that route, but us not being an official couple—it'd be confusing for the baby." Not to mention the grown-ups.

"Sure," she said, her voice small and muffled against his chest. "I understand."

Hand beneath her chin, he tipped her head up. "Do you? Really? Because I'm afraid you're going to take this personally. Just because I have issues, doesn't mean that if I didn't, I wouldn't marry you in a heartbeat. You're a really great girl. The best. In fact, I—"

"Stop," she said. "All the explanations in the world aren't going to make things better between us." She released a sharp laugh. "And what the hell? Now that you know all my secrets, you might as well know one more."

"What?"

"That I think you're a coward, Adam Logue. I think if you were half the man I've built you up to be, you'd march down to that shrink and demand she stop pussyfooting around and get to the crux of your problem."

"If it'd be that simple, don't you think I'd have already tried?"

"No. Because it *is* that simple. Only it's easier to keep sticking your head in the sand, pretending we're just friends to alleviate your guilt over the fact that in every way but the fun ones—like sleeping together and waking up in each other's arms—we practically *are* married. You're at my condo most every night of the week. We share most every meal. We watch the same TV shows."

"Because we're friends and—"

"Shh!" she said, tugging his arm. "Get down."

"What's wrong?" he whispered.

"See that light over there?" She pointed to the faint glow of headlights through the trees.

"Where's your radio?" he asked.

"In the car."

"Mine, too. Come on." He took her hand for the short run back to the SUV. Once inside, Adam tried to contact Caleb or Beau—or for that matter, any member of their team. But as usual with this case, no one responded.

Hand on her door latch, Bug said, "Stay here. I'll

run back to the cabin to let the guys know they have company."

"Good call. Be careful." He caught her stare for a split second longer than was probably necessary. But at the moment, though it went against every oath he'd taken when joining the Marshals Service, he found himself caring more about Bug's safety than the judge's or even his own.

"You, too," she said.

The suspect vehicle steadily came closer, and Adam secured his bulletproof vest, then reached for his gun and a spotlight. Adrenaline pumping, from his vantage in the center of the dirt road, he soon made out a late-model Ford pickup.

Upon seeing him, the vehicle's driver stopped, leaned out the open window. "Hey, there! Need a hand?"

"No, thank you," Adam said, flashing his silver star. "I'm here on government business. Mind telling me what brings you out here in the middle of the night?"

"Goin' fishin'," the balding, elderly man said. "This is the public access road to Big Bear Lake, isn't it?"

"No, sir. I'm afraid you made a wrong turn about five miles back. This is a private road."

"Oh," the man said with seemingly genuine surprise. "Sorry to be of trouble. I'll just head the other way."

"Thank you, sir. Hope you catch some big ones."

"Me, too."

Adam flinched when the guy reached for something, but relaxed to see it was only a thermos mug filled with coffee. He knew, because the smell had him craving a cup. Along with an entire coffee cake.

A few minutes later all that remained of the fisherman's visit was lingering dust.

Not a good thing, considering that once again Adam was left with nothing to do but feel lousy over the way things had gone down with Bug.

Speaking of which, she headed toward him, the soles of her boots crunching gravel.

"You're not going to believe this," she said.

He groaned. "What now?"

"I caught every one of those guys napping. The only one up was your dad."

"My dad? What's he doing here?"

"Wanna take a stab at what he was doing?"

Adam raised his eyebrows. "Raiding the fridge?"

She shook her head. "Talking on his cell. You win a trip to Disneyland if you guess who he was talking with."

"Franks?"

She laughed. "Victoria. Allie's mother."

"As in, Caleb's wife's mother?"

"Ding, ding, ding." She'd reached him and stood with her hands on her hips. "Who was our guest?"

"Lost fisherman."

"Something's not right here."

"Want me to call Franks?"

"No, I think someone like Gillian might have more answers."

"Huh?" He wrinkled his nose. "What's my sister going to know about any of this?"

"Humor me," Bug said, and reached for her phone.

FIFTEEN MINUTES LATER Charity slammed her phone shut, then couldn't decide if she was furious, humiliated or both.

"Well?" Adam asked. "She tell you anything?"

"More like *everything*. Can you believe this whole setup is a scam?"

"Huh?" He scratched his head.

"Your father and Franks cooked this up. Apparently they think we make a cute couple, and thought all we needed for nature to take its course was for us to spend a lot of late-night time alone."

"But we're supposed to be on duty. And why is Suck-up Sam here? Everyone knows the guy has the hots for you and he makes my teeth hurt just looking at him."

"Maybe they're really trying to fix me up with him?" she asked, finding it oddly liberating that Adam finally knew the way she felt.

"Don't go there," he said, fury in his every step as he marched toward the judge's cabin.

"Oh," she said, falling into step behind him. "So you won't have me, but no other man can, either?"

"I didn't say that."

"Then what are you saying?"

"Hell, I don't know. Just, please, don't go out with that guy. It'd kill me."

"What do you think it did to me?" Charity said. "Hearing all about your big night on the town with a Puerto Rican swimsuit model?"

"Touché." He stopped, slipped his hands around her waist and kissed her hard, dizzying her with need and wanting for more than drive-by kisses and endless teasing talk. "I'm sorry about that. It won't happen again."

"Okay, stop," she said, palms on his chest, pushing him away. "One minute, you're practically calling me your property, and the next, you're telling me—"

It was hard to speak, let alone think when he was kissing her again. This time, incredibly soft and sweet and gentle with a sweep of his tongue that made her knees weak and stomach tipsy. When he stopped for air, he rested his forehead against hers. Sighed. "I can't promise you anything, Charity, but if you'll bear with me…I don't know, maybe I can try."

"Try what?" she asked, hardly hearing her words over her runaway pulse. "Admitting what we share already goes beyond mere friendship?"

Pads of his thumbs over her lips, he nodded. His warm breath fanned her mouth and nose, and she drank him in. His smell and flavor. Root beer. And Adam, all Adam. "I do love you," he said. "But

I don't know if that's enough. I'm sick inside, and I—" His words caught in his throat and her heart went out to him, wishing she hadn't caused him to have to face his demoned past, yet in the same breath knowing if he didn't, there'd never be a shot at the two of them ending up together.

"Shh…" she murmured, lips cautiously against his. "I think we've both said enough for tonight."

"Then what do you want to do?" he asked.

"I'll tell you one thing," she said with a wide grin. "It doesn't involve going anywhere near the judge's cabin."

"I NEVER THOUGHT our first time would be on a bunk bed," Adam said, fingers fumbling with Charity's bra clasp.

"So then you've thought about us doing this sort of thing?" she asked. "Before now? And that time we drank too much wine with my lousy dinner?"

"Morning, noon and night," he said, finally freeing her breasts, exposing them to the cold night air, then to his hot moist tongue. He suckled her slow and hard and with enough rhythm to leave her knowing the best was yet to come. "And your dinner wasn't *that* bad."

Moaning and squirming beneath him, she slid her fingers into his hair, tugging, toying with the dark waves she'd so many times ached to explore. "Yes… it was."

"Nope…" He dragged his kisses to her throat, and

she arched her neck, granting him greater access while she skimmed her hands along shoulders even broader than she'd dreamed. "It wasn't... You and your cooking are beautiful." He hovered above her for a moment, then leaned onto his side, smoothing her hair back from her face. "I didn't come prepared. That all right?"

Seeing how Charity wanted nothing more than to have this man's baby, and knowing he'd been safe with the few dates there'd been since Angela, she nodded.

"Wait," she said.

"What?"

"Before we do this, I have to know you're with me. I mean, *really* with me. Here and here..." She touched his forehead then chest.

Sitting back, he pressed her hand over his heart. It pounded beneath her palm. "What do you think? God, Charity, for the first time since—you know—I feel alive. And you did that." He kissed her forehead, then lips. "Sweet, beautiful, entirely too patient, you."

Grinning, scarcely able to contain the joy in her heart, she said, "That's all I needed to know. Please, feel free to proceed."

"Slow or fast?"

"Both."

"Mmm..." he teased, nipping at her earlobe. "I like your style."

From then on, there was no talking, just feeling. Shedding jeans and panties and boxers, they kissed

and explored—sometimes fast, sometimes slow—
Charity felt so exquisitely *right,* there were tears in her
eyes.

And when she felt as if she'd die without having
more of him, she steered him in the right direction,
and as ready as he'd made her, with one, glorious
thrust, he glided right in, gentle. But she raised her
knees, urging him deeper, desperate to quench her
thirst. She loved him. Loved him with every breath
in her body.

Digging her fingers into his back, she cried out for
him, and he for her, and when the dark storm behind
her closed eyes turned white and he shuddered atop
her, then rested his head between her breasts, she
stroked his hair. Petting him. Adoring him. Telling
herself over and over that even though he'd told her
he wasn't capable of making her a lifetime promise,
that no matter what his mouth said, his heart would
soon say something else. Something involving a
wedding and rings and undying, earth-shattering love.

"HEY, WHOA—OH!" Caleb called Saturday morning
on his way into what was supposed to have been the
security team's cabin. Kudos had to go out to his dad.
From its inception, Caleb would've bet big there was
no way this nutty plan to finally get his brother to
admit to loving Charity was going to work, but
judging by the two buck-naked marshals he'd just

walked in on, mission accomplished. "I thought you two were on duty."

Call him twisted, but Caleb had always loved seeing folks squirm, and Charity and Adam were especially comical scrambling for quilts from where they'd lain on blankets in front of the now-cold stone hearth.

"You could've knocked," Adam said.

"Yeah, but aren't you two supposed to be guarding the road?"

"Like you've been guarding the judge?" Charity asked, quilt up to her neck, eyebrows raised, hair thoroughly mussed. "We're on to to you, Caleb. Gillian spilled your whole dirty scheme."

"No way."

She nodded. "Yes, way."

"That's it," Caleb said. "For having such a big mouth, she's off my Christmas list."

"This was low," Adam said. "Even for you."

"Hey…" Hand to his chest, playing innocent, Caleb said, "It was Dad's idea. I just rode along for the beer and poker."

"And where'd you get the judge?"

"He's an old college buddy of Dad's. Good sport for letting us use his cabins."

Adam threw a pillow at him, but missed.

"So?" Caleb asked. "Ready to set a date?"

"For what?" Adam asked.

"A wedding, you big dope. What'd you think?

You just deflowered the poor girl. The least you could do now is make her an honest woman."

"Ah, I was already deflowered," Charity said, rising, a quilt wrapped sarong-style around her. "Prom night. Hugh Barnes."

"You never told me that," Adam said. He rose, too, with a quilt around his waist.

"You never asked," she retorted just before locking herself in the bathroom.

"You're marrying her," Caleb rumbled under his breath. "And that's final."

"The hell I am," Adam said. "And who appointed you boss of my life?"

"Dammit, Adam. The girl's sweet as cotton candy. She adores you, and to be honest, at the moment, the whole family—myself included—likes her a whole helluva lot more than you."

"Gee, thanks," Adam said from in front of the fridge. He pulled out a pack of hot dogs and shoved four into his mouth.

Caleb marched to his side, snatching one for himself. "What's wrong with you, man? What kind of games are you playing? Dad brought us up better than that."

Adam rolled his eyes.

"I'm not fooling around. I know you've been seeing a shrink, and that she thinks the solution to your problem is seeing other women, but personally I think that's a crock. All you really need is—"

"Peace and quiet," his brother said from the foot of the bunk bed where he was pulling on his jeans. "Catch you later, bro."

Barefoot with no shirt on, Adam headed for the great outdoors.

"Don't you walk out on—" Too late. Adam had already slammed the door.

"Coast clear?" Charity asked, creaking open the bathroom door.

"Relatively."

She beelined for the crumpled black jeans and T-shirt piled on the floor.

"If it helps," he said, "we're all rooting for you."

"What would help," she said, cradling her clothes to her chest on the way back to the bathroom, "is for you and everyone else to stay out of this."

"But we want you two to finally tie the knot. Lord knows, you already act like an old married couple. Don't you think it's high time you made it official?"

The only reply Caleb got was a slammed bathroom door.

Chapter Ten

"Sorry about that," Adam said to Bug from his perch on a lakeside boulder. The morning was cloudless and still. The lake, a mirror reflecting age-old firs taller than his apartment building. "Caleb was out of line."

"Was he?" she asked, joining him on the rock.

He shot her a dirty look. "You can't be serious? You think this strong-arm tactic of my family's to throw us together is cool?"

"That's not what I meant," she said, hand on his forearm. "True, most of what they've done was a bit heavy-handed."

"A bit?" Adam winced.

"All I'm saying is that whether we end up together, or not, you need help. You're letting your past determine your future, and it's not healthy—for either of us, seeing how I've pretty much pinned my future on you."

"Wish you wouldn't," Adam said. She looked so pretty in the morning sun. Even wearing jeans and a sweatshirt, her hair a mess and no makeup, she was stunning in a simple, wholesome way.

"I wish I could not think about you, too," she said softly, staring out at the lake. "There are times I wish I'd never even met you."

"Would it help if I filed for a transfer?"

"I used to think so." She swallowed hard, and when she finally did look at him, her eyes shone with unshed tears.

"What do you want me to do? Name it and I'll do it."

She laughed through tears she no longer bothered to hold back.

"Don't cry," he said. "*Please* don't cry. I'll marry you, okay? Just name the day and time and I'll be there."

His offer only made her cry harder.

"D-don't you get it?" she said. "I'd be lying if I said I didn't want to marry you, Adam, but what would be the point? Two, three, ten years down the road, after we've brought kids into the world, you decide you're still hung up on the past. Still harboring guilt over Angela's death or still in love with her or whatever. What happens when those feelings eat you alive, and we wind up in an ugly divorce? Sorry," she said with a brittle laugh, "but that's not my idea of a good time."

"So where do we go from here?" Adam asked, scared he was on the verge of losing the best thing to ever happen to him, and all because of…what?

Standing, Bug said, "I'm going to grab my stuff and catch a ride home with Sam and Bear."

Adam squeezed his eyes shut tight. "Caleb or Beau will take you. Please not Sam."

He opened his eyes to find her staring at him with a look of disgust, pity, loathing. "Doesn't matter how I get there," she said. "I just have to get home."

"Then let me take you." He scrambled to his feet, wincing from the rock's bite on his bare feet.

"That's okay," she said with a halfhearted wave midway through the field leading to the cabin.

He hobbled after her, but then stopped.

What was chasing after her going to do other than hurt more? Bottom line, he knew in his heart he wasn't good enough for her. Period. End of his sad, screwed-up story.

Why couldn't he run after her, pull her into his arms and make her understand why he was so messed up? Why? Because if he didn't even know himself, how the hell was he supposed to explain it to her?

CHARITY SLEPT the whole ride home, thankful she'd called backseat ahead of Bear, who usually hid out in the back playing Tetris on his Game Boy.

In front of her building, Sam hopped out to grab her gear from the storage compartment. Bear was in the front seat, snoring.

"Well, thanks for the ride," she said, reaching for her two bags.

He held tight to them. "Let me see you up. It's the least I can do."

"Thanks, but—"

"I'm seeing you to your door," he said, already headed up the walk.

Too weary to fight him, she followed, opening the door, then, in the small, elegantly furnished lobby, she pressed the elevator's up button.

The ride was tense.

The moment in front of her door when she went fishing for her key, a thousand times worse.

"I'm sorry about what went down out there," he said. "I went along strictly for the poker. For the record, I never wanted to see you with Adam. The guy's a head case. You deserve better."

"Funny," she said, shooting him a half smile. "He says the same thing about himself—and you."

"Thereby proving my point. Rest up," he said, setting her bags in front of the door. "Then have dinner with me later."

"Thanks, but…" She shook her head.

"Come on," he urged. "One dinner. It's all-you-can-eat-prime-rib night at Ziggy's. I'll even help you make sense of whatever it is you're feeling for Adam."

"Okay," she said, fitting the key in her lock. "But strictly as friends—and mostly because drowning myself in prime rib sounds like heaven." Yes, seeing how her dream of not only procreating with, but marrying Adam would never come true, she needed to get on with finding the real man with whom she was destined to live out her life. Deep in her heart of hearts, she knew Sam wasn't the one. *The one* would have to cause happy butterflies in her stomach. Kind of like the ones she'd experienced while she and Adam had made love.

"Great," Sam said with a little clap. "Pick you up at seven?"

"I'll meet you there."

"Fair enough." He winked. "It's a date."

"No, Sam, it's just dinner between—" The elevator dinged and he stepped on. "Friends," she finished out of principle. "We're *just* friends."

Door open, Charity kicked her bags inside, then collapsed on the sofa, glowering at the gorgeous Mount Hood view.

The day was sheer perfection. Bright sun, the temperature in the mid-seventies. Not a breath of wind. The rest of Portland was biking or hiking or just lounging in the sun like lazy turtles. All of which she should've been doing, trying to keep busy to keep her mind off of Adam. Off of the amazing feel of his hands and mouth on her—

No good, she thought, reaching for the phone.

Charity tried her sister at home, and eventually reached her on her cell. Steph answered on the third ring. "Sis," she gushed. "I'm so glad you called. I was just about to call you, but—" Her voice sounded muffled for a second, and in the background there was laughing and chatter and clinking and jubilant classical music. "Sorry," she said, back on the line. "Dr. Larry's cousin Helen's leaving, and I wanted to give her a proper goodbye. Oh, Charity, you're never going to believe what this amazing man did for me. First, on a dawn hot-air balloon ride, floating past Mount Hood, he proposed. Then, once we had our feet back on the ground, he caught me completely off guard with a gorgeous surprise engagement party. Absolutely everyone we know is here, except you. Larry wanted to call you, but with you being up north on a case and all—"

"It's okay," Charity said. "I understand. And I'm thrilled for you. Really."

"Where are you? We're at Larkspur Junction at that sweet B and B. It's on the main drag through town. You can't miss it. Why don't you drive down?"

"Thanks—" Charity crossed her fingers "—but I'm still in Cedarville. It sounds fun, but just isn't feasible."

"All right," Steph said in a pouty tone. "But I miss you."

"I miss you, too. Congratulations." Charity turned off her phone, then settled in for a long afternoon of self-pity. Who'd have thought both Caldwell girls would be proposed to on the same morning?

Had Charity been stupid to not take Adam up on his offer? True it hadn't been sincere, but with time, who knew? Maybe it could've all somehow worked out.

On her way to the shower, she snort-laughed.

"YOU'RE LATE," Sam said as Charity slipped into the booth at Ziggy's that she usually shared with Adam.

"Sorry. There was a wreck on Boulder and Lincoln. Had to take the long way around."

"Not a problem," he said. "Sounds like you need a beer."

"Two or three," she said with a grin. "But seeing how I'm my own designated driver, better stick with iced tea."

"Sure?" he asked. "Dinner will take at least an hour or two. Plus, I hear Ziggy's launching his first karaoke night on this very evening. Meaning you're in for a treat." He winked.

"Oh, yeah?" Already knowing what she wanted to order, she slipped her menu to the table's edge. "What're you going to sing?"

"It's a toss-up between 'New York, New York' and 'Every Breath You Take' by the Police."

"Interesting choices," she said just before the waitress appeared.

"Where's your usual sidekick?" Nancy asked.

"Beats me," Charity said with a disinterested shrug.

"Ooooooh," Nancy said. "Lover's quarrel."

"We're not—" Charity had been on the verge of fighting the lovers comment, but seeing how they now were officially lovers, what was the point? "Um, when you get a chance, I'll have iced tea and the all-you-can-eat special."

"You got it," she said, taking Sam's order, then hustling off to another table.

"Logue's a first-class jerk for what he's putting you through. If you were mine," Sam said, reaching for her hand, "I'd treat you like a princess. You'd for sure never be at loose ends on a Saturday night."

"Don't," she said, too emotionally shattered to even bother looking him in the eyes. "Please, just don't."

"Sorry, but it needs to be said. I'm only—"

"One more word," she said with a slight lift of her chin, "and I'm out the door."

"Fair enough." He grinned. "So? It was a gorgeous day. You get a chance to get out and enjoy all that sun?"

ADAM SAUNTERED into Ziggy's and groaned to hear the warbling coming from the newly installed stage just to the right of the bar. Great. Just freakin' great.

He'd come in here for solace. A few slabs of prime rib. A few beers. A few quarters of football, basketball or ping-pong. Didn't much matter what the sport was, just so long as it got his mind off last night. Holding Charity. Kissing her, easing into her.

Losing his soul to her.

"Long time no see!" Nancy called from behind the bar. "Charity's already in your usual booth if you're meeting her!"

No way.

Eyes closed, rubbing his forehead, Adam was on the verge of leaving when out of the corner of his eye he caught a blood-curdling sight he'd no doubt carry to his grave.

Bug wasn't alone in *their* booth, but with Sam. And she was laughing over something Suck-up had said.

Growling low in his throat, it was all Adam could do not to march over there and drag her caveman-style back to his apartment where he'd—

What? Make love to her again? Heck, yeah.

But then what? Would they spend the night together only to wake up to another awkward morning like this one? To more circular talk and logic that endlessly made him out to be the bad guy and her a saint.

Didn't matter that she was saint, he thought, easing into a corner booth with a too-good view of his most despised enemy and the woman he loved but didn't deserve.

Nancy sauntered over, order pad in one hand, draft beer in her other. "Looks like you've had better days."

He downed half the beer. "Better decades."

"Okay, let's hear it," she said with a grunt, sliding onto the seat across from him. "What's up between you and the cutie you're normally hanging with?" She nodded in Bug's direction.

"Got a week?"

"More like two minutes."

"Then I'll give you the highlight reel. Girl says she loves boy. Boy thinks he loves girl, but isn't quite sure how to tell for certain, and then proceeds to thoroughly screw himself out of any chance of living happily ever after."

"Oh, I wouldn't say that," Nancy said.

"Look at them." He jerked his thumb their direction. "Laughing it up. She's having the time of her life."

"*Humph.* Ever occur to you she's a little too happy? Trust me, it's an act. Five seconds before you walked in the room, her chin was lower than Ziggy's bar revenues since putting in that damned karaoke machine."

He laughed, but the slight lift in spirits didn't last long as Suck-up mounted the stage.

"Test," Sam said into the microphone, tapping it a couple times. "Testing, one, two."

"Here we go," Nancy said, rolling her eyes. "This is his third number. But I have to admit, he's pretty good."

"At barking," Adam muttered under his breath.

Nancy slid out of the booth. Patting his back, she said, "I'll be right out with your Saturday-night usual."

As Sam launched into some sappy boy band ballad, Adam stole a glance at Charity. She was beautiful. He wanted her. Now. But through his own stupid insecurities and hang-ups, he'd put her under a glass case he didn't have the foggiest idea how to break.

She must've felt his stare, as she looked his way.

At first, she lurched, as if just the sight of him had

startled her. But then she winked, as if the two of them were in on some big secret. Only for the life of him he didn't know what it was.

But he was about to find out…

While Sam was still crooning, Adam moseyed on over to his usual booth and his usual dinner companion.

"Hey," he said, easing onto the seat beside her.

"Hey."

"What'd you do all day?" he asked, snagging one of her home fries.

"Truth? Moped."

"Yeah," he said. "Me, too. Wanna get out of here? Talk?"

"Yep."

"Great, let's go."

"I want to," she said. "But I'm not going to. I adore you, Adam, but there comes a point in every girl's love life when self-preservation has to kick in. For my own sanity, I can't hang out with you anymore. Share prime rib, beer or football with you. I have to quit you. Cold turkey."

Sam finished his song and Bug burst into applause.

"Great job," she said when he got back to the booth. "You've got real talent."

He shrugged. "Mom made me take five years of singing lessons before I finally convinced Dad to talk her into letting me quit."

"You should've kept going," she said with a

dainty sip of her tea. "You might've been the next American Idol."

It was all Adam could do not to barf. Was Bug even listening to herself?

"What time did you get back into town?" Sam asked.

"Sixish. Caleb, Beau and Dad insisted on spending the afternoon fishing."

"Sounds fun," Sam said. "Catch anything?"

"Don't know," Adam said, helping himself to another of Bug's fries, hoping Suck-up got the hint. The fries were his, and so was the woman. "I napped. It was a long night."

Bug kicked him under the table.

"Ouch," he said. "What'd you do that for?"

"Come on," she said to Sam, grabbing her purse. "Let's go."

"You sure?" he asked.

She nodded, shot Adam one last dirty look, then left the bar.

"BUG!" ADAM HOLLERED outside her condo two hours and roughly eight beers later—he'd lost count somewhere around five.

"Hush," she said, fumbling with the chain lock. "You want old Mrs. Kleypus to call the police?"

"I drank too much," he said.

"I can smell." Stepping aside for him to enter, she waved her hand in front of her nose. "You didn't drive over here, did you?"

"Nope. I was a good boy and took a cab. Sam here?" he asked, doing a quick search of the kitchen, bedroom and bath.

"No, he's not," she said, chasing after him, catching up at the foot of her bed. "And you shouldn't be, either."

"I live here," he said.

"No, Adam, you don't."

"But I want to," he said, hands on her shoulders, angling in for a kiss.

She scrambled away from him. "No, you don't," she reminded him. "You want to live where you were with Angela, remember?"

"Oh, yeah." Sitting hard on the edge of the bed, he scratched his head. "Only after you left Ziggy's, I got to thinking about that, and maybe I like it here better."

"You are so wasted," she said. "If I had half a brain, I'd call security and have them kick your butt to the curb."

"But you love me and want to take care of me, right?"

"Half right. Come on," she said, lugging him to his feet. "Sofa City for you, my friend."

"But I like the bed better," he whined.

"Then maybe next time you should crash at Frederika's condo."

He snorted. "That was funny. You're funny. I love you lots."

"Yeah, yeah," Charity said. "Just keep heading for the sofa."

He landed with a thud, then she helped him lower his head down and feet up, waving away his boozy-smoky smell.

"Off with your shoes," she said, fighting flashbacks of what else she'd helped him take off just last night. After shoving her ladybug pillow under his head, she took a pink afghan Aunt Bedelia crocheted for her sixteenth birthday and spread it over him. Tall as he was, though, it only covered his chest to his shins.

"There you go," she said. "See you in the morning."

"Bug?" he asked just as she turned out the sofa table lamp.

"Yeah?"

"You should be called, *Buglicious* 'cause you're a very *booyootiful* woman."

She rolled her eyes.

"Know what else?"

"What?" she made the mistake of asking on her way into the bedroom.

"I love you. I *really* love you. And I've been a fool up till now, but not anymore. I might've had ten beers—maybe twelve—but I've never thought more clearly. Beyond any shadow of *doubtedness,* you are for sure the woman for me."

"Uh-huh," she said, flicking off the hall light, too.

"When the sun comes up," he said, "I'm going to prove how much I love you."

"I'll look forward to that," she said just before shutting her bedroom door. "Good night."

Chapter Eleven

Charity woke to masculine singing in the shower. Unlike Sam, this man couldn't sing two notes in tune, let alone a whole song—currently a number faintly reminiscent of something Pearl Jam might've sung, but she couldn't be sure.

The water turned off, and she flopped onto her side and pulled up the covers. She couldn't bear another scene with Adam. She shouldn't have even let him spend the night, but seeing how he'd been in no shape to travel, she hadn't had much choice.

Well… Had she truly wanted him gone, she could've called a cab—or for that matter, made good on her threat to call security, but both those plans had seemed harsh.

Whistling now instead of singing, heavy footfalls told her he'd left the bathroom and was on his way to the kitchen or living room. Knowing Adam, the former as opposed to the latter.

Rolling onto her back, staring at the ceiling, she

tried ignoring the woodsy scent of the soap and shampoo he kept at her place in case he wanted to shower after work.

Up at the lake, after they'd made love, they'd showered together. Standing naked against him, all soapy-slick had been heaven. Like something out of a hazy dream, she couldn't quite be sure if it had truly happened or not.

"Good morning, sleepyhead." Adam appeared, breakfast tray in hand, loaded with French toast and coffee and sliced strawberries and bananas.

"Hey," she said, sitting up in bed. "Wow, what's the occasion?"

"Can't a guy make a meal for his favorite girl?"

"Please, don't," she said, taking the napkin from the tray to put it on her lap. "I hate it when you do that."

"What?" He perched on the edge of the bed and popped a berry into his mouth.

"You know what, Adam. Throwing out false platitudes. Just like when checkout clerks tell you to have a nice day, they don't mean it. They're just following store policy."

"First," he said, borrowing her fork for a bite of French toast. "I don't take kindly to being called a liar. I mean what I say. And second, maybe you, Miss Negative, don't mean it when you tell others to have a nice day, but lots of other folks do."

"You know what I'm getting at," she said, taking back her fork. "Stop saying things you don't mean."

"Who says I don't?"

"Mom always said that if I don't have anything nice to say, then I should keep my mouth shut, but in this case, I can't hold back.

"Right now, Adam Logue, I despise you. I hate you for playing with my emotions this way. For this up/down ride you take me on every single day. I've told you repeatedly to get out of my life and stay out, but that doesn't work. I've made love to you, thinking maybe that would be the incentive you need to once and for all figure out what you want. But you know what? I'm fresh out of ways to deal with you. Every signal you send is conflicting. Same with every word you say. On the one hand, yesterday morning you pretty much made it clear that while we can be close friends or lovers, we'll never be man and wife. In practically the same breath, you ask me to marry you, but with no feeling behind the words. You ask as if inviting me along on a death march."

"I know all that," he said. "And I'm sorry."

"Are you, Adam? Because I'm really starting to wonder if you just like the intrigue of it. Of never really knowing where we stand. You mentioned once that with Angela, you never felt you were good enough for her. Maybe with me, you're wondering am I good enough for you?" She looked into his eyes and quietly asked, "Tell me what you want from me."

"I don't know," he said, plowing his fingers

through his hair. "Don't you think if I did know I'd tell you? Don't you think this is just as hard on me? One minute, I think the two of us might have a legitimate shot at working things out. Then, I think of how I failed Angela. Part of me is scared to death that if I allow myself to love you to that degree, something is going to happen to you. Something totally out of my control. And what then? What if we have kids? How do I tell a little girl the spitting image of you that her mommy's gone? How do I tell a son with your eyes and penchant for bug collecting you're never coming back?"

"Now, you're being silly and melodramatic," she said.

"Am I?" He laughed, "I sure never thought about death when my mom died, but look what happened. It happened again with Angela."

"Yeah, and the odds of the same thing happening with me are insane. Incalculable."

"You so sure?"

"Aggghh!" Setting the tray aside, she pounded his back. "Arguing with you is like arguing with a rock. Like it or not, we're all going to die someday. Not something I care to think about for the next fifty or so years, but a sad fact of life all the same. Now, the question you have to ask yourself is, are you going to spend the next fifty years with one foot in the grave or are you going to start living?"

"Why are you being mean?"

"Mean? Dammit, Adam, I'm being honest. If you had half a brain instead of a peanut in your head, you'd admit I'm right."

With a disgusted sigh, he grabbed the tray, then took off toward the kitchen.

"Yeah, run away," she hollered after him. "Real mature!"

"Oh!" he snapped. "Like it's been mature of you to keep sending me packing every time the conversation doesn't go your way?"

Grabbing the nearest pillow, she buried her face in it. Adam was scared to death to commit. Had she been through the trauma that he had, she couldn't in all honesty say she wouldn't have a few additional issues of her own. But the fact of the matter was that she didn't know for sure how he felt. She could only guess. And judging by his most recent reaction, she'd hit a sore spot.

Bottom line, she wanted a baby—and a husband to go along with tiny him or her. To achieve that, she'd once and for all have to make a clean break from Adam. He'd become a drug. One that was growing increasingly more hazardous to her mental health.

"Sorry about leaving you with the dishes," he said, suddenly appearing at her bedroom door. "But I've gotta run."

"Where?"

"I've got an emergency session with my shrink."

"YOU'RE FORTUNATE to have caught me," Adam's shrink said, gesturing for him to have a seat. Sad statement about his character—or lack thereof—how he'd never even taken the time to remember her name. The plaque on her desk read, Dr. Margaret Davey. "I was just on my way out for a marathon spending spree at my favorite bookstore."

"Sounds hot," he said.

She winked. "When you have a date as gorgeous as mine, it would've been."

"Sorry," he said in what felt like his hundredth apology of the day. He pushed himself out of the quicksand lounge chair. "Had I known you were—"

"Sit down," she said. "My guy knows me well enough to realize that when I get a closemouthed patient like you actually wanting to open up, my mind wouldn't have been much on our date anyway. Now, Mr. Logue, to what do I owe the pleasure of this urgent session?"

"If it'll help," he said, "you can call me Adam."

"All right, Adam." She leaned forward and with steepled hands asked, "What seems to be the problem?"

He outlined the events of the past week, during which she didn't say a word. Just sat there letting him dig a deeper hole.

"My," she said when he topped off his story with the events of that morning. "You have been a busy beaver."

"Well?" he asked, hoping he'd adequately contained the panic lacing his voice. It didn't matter that his initial visits to her had been about satisfying his dad and Franks. Now, Adam wanted this therapy for himself. "Is there hope for me, Doc? Because I really do care an awful lot for Bug, I just—"

"First off," she said with a kind smile. "You're overthinking your perceived problems. Which are— and feel free to jump in and correct me if I'm wrong—fear of *Bug's* mortality. Fear of your own mortality. Fear of not being at the top of your game where your job is concerned. And the big daddy of them all, fear of commitment because you're afraid loving another woman might be all the catalyst fate needs to kill again. How's that? Did I at least hit the highlights?"

"Pretty much," he mumbled, mouth dry, heart pounding.

"Okay," she said, setting her ever-present clipboard on the floor beside her chair. "I've got good news and bad. Which do you want first?"

"Oh, honey," Steph said Sunday afternoon at her house, pulling Charity into a hug. "I'm so sorry. Here I've been yammering about how happy Larry and I are, and you've been through hell."

"I wouldn't exactly call it *hell*," Charity said, remembering the most arousing details of Saturday morning. "Just…" She brushed tears from the corners of her eyes.

Steph went back to clucking and hugging. "I feel like all of this is somehow my fault," she said, smoothing Charity's short hair, guiding her to the sofa. "If only I'd left you alone. At least then you were happy."

"No, I wasn't," Charity said. "On the surface maybe, but deep down, I wasn't any better off than I am now."

"But at least then, you didn't harbor illusions about you and Adam ending up together."

"Yes, I did. I just never mentioned it."

"What're you going to do now?" her sister asked.

"First, I suppose I should talk Franks into transferring me to another office."

"Oh, Charity, no. Why do you have to move? Can't you and Adam just agree to an amicable split?"

Charity laughed. "That's just it. We were never even officially together, which is why it's going to be that much harder to break up."

"THIS IS GOOD," Adam said to Gillian Sunday night at her and Joe's dinner table—thankfully the one in the small dining room. The Medieval-themed dining hall, they reserved for special occasions. Her beef stew hit the spot on what'd turned into a bitterly cold, dreary night. Rain pelted the dark picture windows at a nearly horizontal slant. Their girls, Meggie and Chrissy, were already in bed. "Since when did you learn to cook like this?"

Joe cleared his throat. "Since I cooked it for her."

"That's so not true," she said with a playful swat to his shoulder. "I helped—a lot. I chopped potatoes and celery and—"

"Just kidding," he said, planting a kiss on top of her head. To Adam he added, "Dinner was a team effort."

"However it came together," Adam said, helping himself to thirds, slipping their dog Barney a chunk of beef, "I like it."

Gillian and Joe talked kids while Adam served up one last scoop. Nothing like a good, hearty meal to get his mind off—

"Adam," Gillian said. "You ever going to tell us why you're here, other than to eat us out of house and home?"

He looked up from his latest spoonful. "Can't a guy miss his sister?"

"Not after the weekend he's just had."

"Caleb and Beau have big mouths."

"Don't forget dear, old Dad," she quipped.

"It wasn't that big a deal."

"Right," she said. "I didn't think so."

Dinner wound down, and so did Adam's courage.

He shouldn't have come here. Joe and Gillian had problems of their own what with trying to raise two kids and mow the lawn of the mausoleum they called a house.

Adam helped with the dishes, downed three slices of chocolate-cream pie, then was just getting ready to track down his coat when Dr. Margaret's words came back to haunt him, as did the real reason why he'd found himself at his sister and brother-in-law's.

I've got good news and bad.... The bad is that we're all going to die. The good, is that we're all going to die. Meaning, we're blessed with a finite amount of time with which to live our dreams. Your clock is ticking, Adam Logue. Whether you use those ticks or throw them away trying to fix things that can never be undone is entirely up to you.

"Gil," Adam said as she played mother hen by zipping his leather coat, "you mind if I have a few minutes alone with Joe?"

She raised her eyebrows, but motioned toward an endless hall, off of which Joe's study could be found. "His overseas conference call should be over any minute now. Take all the time you need. I'm going to check on the kids, then hit the sack." After kissing him on the cheek, Gillian climbed the stairs, leaving Adam on his own to ponder the wisdom of what he was about to do.

With lead in his stomach and feet, he started the long walk to Joe and, hopefully, answers.

A minute later he knocked on one of a set of double doors. "Joe?" he called.

"Come on in," his brother-in-law said, voice muffled.

In a dark, wood-paneled room with large-scale

leather furniture, books and more computer equipment than most office supply stores, Adam found Joe seated behind a desk bigger than Bug's Bug. Barney was sacked out in front of a crackling fire.

"What's up?" Joe asked. "Gil called down and said you wanted to talk to me?"

Shaking his head, Adam said, "Secrets and this family don't do real well together."

Grinning, holding out a pricey-looking box of cigars, Joe asked, "Smoke?"

"No, thanks."

"Mind if I do?"

"Not at all."

Cigar in hand, Joe stepped out from behind his desk and led Adam to a pair of wing chairs in front of the fire. Once they'd sat for a few minutes, Adam savoring aged bourbon, Joe, his cigar, Joe said, "I've got a fair idea of what you want to discuss."

"Oh?" Adam said.

"My wife. My *first* wife. Meggie's mom." He stood, took a photo album from a row lining one of the room's many shelves. "Have a look," he said, handing it to Adam who opened the cover only to be blown away by a movie-star-gorgeous blonde. Pages and pages of her smiling and laughing and holding Meggie and Barney and Joe.

Seeing his brother-in-law so happy like this with another woman left Adam more confused than ever. Even a little angry, as though he'd been punched. As though to even have these tangible memories in the home he shared with Adam's sister was somehow adulterous.

"Seems like another lifetime," Joe said. "When I lost Willow, there were days I wished to die. But there was Meggie. Always Meggie."

"I don't know what to say," Adam said. "I knew you'd been married before, but…"

"It was easier to believe Willow and I had a bad marriage? That she was an old crone and back then I'd had a beer belly and Meggie had been a sassy brat? And then I met your sister and she made everything all better?"

"No. Hell, no, man. That's not what I meant at all."

"I know," Joe said with a puff of his cigar. "I know. See that?" He pointed to a photo of Willow and Meggie hamming for the camera while in the midst of baking. Meggie couldn't have been much more than two and both mother and child were covered in flour. "Willow was an amazing cook. She could whip up ambrosia from cardboard and paste. I loved her so much that after she'd died, it sometimes hurt to breathe. One minute she was there and the next…"

"You don't have to do this," Adam said.

"I know. But when I look at you, a lot of times, I see myself—only worse. After she…well, after Willow was gone, I ran away. Didn't talk to hardly anyone but my dog—and the fact that I'm still referring to that mutt as a person should tell you just what a fix I was in." He chuckled, but there was no happiness in his eyes. Only pain. "You, on the other hand, have never shown any outward signs of grief. The day after Angela's death, you were back at work."

"Damned straight—nailing the bastard who shot her."

"Yet even after you'd done just that, you kept working. And working. In fact, the whole time I've known you, I can't recall you ever having taken more than a weekend away from your job."

"Sure, I have," he said, swirling the amber liquid in his glass. "Remember? Right after San Francisco."

"How could I have forgotten? A swell break from the monotony for you."

"For what he did to Gracie, Vicente deserved to die. Two weeks' mandatory leave. Small price to pay for the pleasure of seeing that bastard dead."

"The fact that you did that—shot him between the eyes without a moment's hesitation, is what landed you in trouble. Since losing Angela, you've become like a machine. The only time Gillian and I ever see you soften is when you're with Charity. She's good for you. Reminds you what it's like to be human. Which brings us right back around to the real reason you're here, which I'm assuming isn't to rifle through my past, but ask me how I let go of it."

Chapter Twelve

"I'm not letting you in," Charity said to Adam outside her condo at one in the morning.

"Come on," he said, "I know it's late. And I apologize for that. Truly, but what I have to say can't wait."

She sighed, and against her better judgment stepped aside to let Adam back into her world. But he'd better make it quick. Having already made the decision that from now on they were co-workers—nothing more—she wouldn't go back on her word. Even if it was only to herself.

"Five minutes," she said. "That's how much time you have till I'm going back to bed."

"Fair enough," he said, dragging her by her sweatshirt sleeve to the sofa. "Bug—*Charity*—my head's spinning. There's so much I want to tell you, I'm not even sure where to begin."

"For starters, are you drunk?"

"Sober as a church mouse."

Nose wrinkled, she asked, "Sure that's how the saying goes?"

"Does it matter?" he asked, reaching for her hands. "Charity, I'm cured. I had this long talk with my shrink, and then Joe, and they both told me it's okay for me to love you. That I'm not jinxed or cursed. That it's all right for me to be happy again. Live a full life."

He pulled her into his arms and kissed her, kissed her till she quivered from his warm breath and achingly familiar smell. She loved him, Lord help her, she loved him. But did he honestly believe what he was saying? "Adam, sweetheart, no one—or two— people could solve all your problems in one day."

"I know, but listen," he said, cupping his hands to her cheeks, searching deep into her eyes. "Joe said the most amazing thing. That I don't have to be afraid anymore. I don't have to worry about disrespecting Angela's memory. I just have to love her as she was. You know, cherish the memory, but not devote my every thought to it. Joe and my shrink reminded me that if Angela truly loved me she wouldn't have wanted me to die with her. And I've been dying, you know. My dad saw it, and brothers and even you, but I didn't listen. Until you, I was— Oh, Charity." Her cheeks still framed by his hands, he seized her lips in another kiss. A deeper, mesmerizing sharing of emotions. "I loved her," he said. "But she's gone, and here you are. Like this shining beacon, showing me the way. I love you, I love you, I—"

"I'm sorry, Adam. Please don't take this person-ally, but I think I'm going to be—" She made a mad dash for the bathroom and promptly threw up.

"You okay?" Adam asked ten minutes later, cold rag on Charity's forehead once the worst of whatever malady had bit her had passed.

She nodded, and he helped her up and into bed.

"This wasn't quite how I'd planned the night to go," he said, easing beside her, brushing her hair back from her cool forehead.

"Must've been something I ate," she said. "I've been starving all day, but now…" She blanched. "I never want to eat again."

"That's okay," he said. "You don't have to eat, just tell me we'll get through this together. That any more rough patches I have, you'll help me through."

"Hey," she complained, rolling onto her side to face him. "Who's helping who here? I'm the sick one, remember?"

"Sorry," he said. "Back to you, is there anything I can get you? Water? Sprite?"

"The one thing you could do for me, Adam, is reassure me that all the pretty words you just spouted were for real. I'd just made the decision to make a clean break from you, but here you are again, telling me things have changed. I won't play this constant hot-cold game. I can't. It's not fair."

"Agreed," he said. "Name anything you want, and I'll give it to you."

Hugging her pillow, she looked away. "Oh, that's easy. But the one thing I want, you're nowhere near ready to give."

"A wedding?" he asked. "Try me. Name a date, and I'm there. Gillian's been dying to have a wedding at her castle. Want to rock her world by tying the knot at Christmas?"

Charity wasn't sure what to make of this new-and-improved Adam. Had one session with his shrink and a heart-to-heart with Joe really done all this?

Though every bone in her body told her not to trust him, that his intoxicating words were but one more trap, she raised her chin, tremulously smiling. "If you hurt me again, Adam Logue…"

"Trust me," he said, planting the most tender kiss ever on her forehead.

And because she loved him, she overrode the nagging voice telling her to slow down and said, "Yes, I would love to marry you for Christmas."

STEPH HAD SCREAMED for joy when Charity told her the news of her and Adam's engagement. As did Adam's sister and sisters-in law. Franks even gave her Monday afternoon off to go wedding-dress shopping. So why, when she should be the happiest woman in the world, was she now in the bathroom of Hearts on Fire Bridal Boutique tossing her cookies? Or more accurately, the chicken salad she'd had for lunch.

"Everything all right in there?" Gregory, her personal bridal assistant, asked discreetly from outside the door. The man was six-four and much prettier than Charity.

"Just dandy!" she sang out, staring at her waxy complexion in an ornately edged gilded mirror.

"Bridal jitters are completely normal," he sang back. "Just get that cute little bootie of yours back out here and we'll pop the cherry on some to-die-for bubbly we just got in this morning."

After splashing cold water on her face, she dried it with a paper towel, then headed back to the trenches. Who'd of thought picking a wedding dress would be so hard?

"It's about time," Gracie said, looking at least fifteen months pregnant in the posh surroundings. Plush white carpet formed a luxurious foundation for funky, gilded Victorian furniture. Every wall surface that wasn't gilded was mirrored. "What you waitin' for?" Gwen Stefani asked from hidden speakers. "We were all starting to worry," Gracie said.

The whole gang was gathered. Gillian, Allie and her mom—even Adam's dad, Vince. All of them were staring at her as if she was some rare form of alien life.

"I'm fine," Charity said. "Really."

"Excellent," Gregory said with a double clap. "On with the show. Michelle, Rochelle, Babette! The bride's ready for her next selections!"

Three women as perfect as that stacked swimsuit

model Adam once dated, paraded around the room
in wedding dresses Charity didn't have half the bod
for—not to mention the confidence.

Who was Charity trying to fool? Even if Adam
had finally proposed, that didn't mean he truly loved
her. All it really meant was that he'd finally caved to
family pressure. Or even worse, that he'd felt so sorry
for her that because of all the years they'd been
friends, he'd for real proposed out of some misguided
sense of duty.

Oh, sure, she'd had the confidence to tell herself she
was over him, but when he came back, proposing with
all the aplomb of a knight in shining armor, all her
carefully constructed emotional walls crumbled. She
wanted a baby. Oh, how she wanted a baby. And she
most especially wanted that baby with Adam, but what
then? Now that it looked as if all of that might really be
happening, what did she do about her job? She'd fought
so hard to be one of the toughest guys around, so what
did it say about her that now, in addition to taking down
bad guys, she also wanted to try out new chocolate-chip
cookie recipes and take the kids to Saturday matinees?

The worst part was, what if she did start an amazing
new chapter of her life, only to have Adam falter yet
again? How would she ever pick up the pieces?

"Oh, that one's gorgeous," Allie's mom, Victoria, gushed.

"I have to agree," Vince said. "That's a real con-
tender."

"Let's add that one to Charity's try-on list," Gillian said in regard to the beaded chiffon dream dress that looked more like a silken sparkling cloud than a garment.

The show went on and on while Charity's stomach continued its nervous dance. After ten more dresses had been added to her try-on pile, the parade finally ended and it was time for her portion of the show.

In the dressing room, Steph asked, "You still under the weather? You don't look so hot."

"Thanks," Charity said, slipping into a sequined-satin number she felt totally out of place even trying on, let alone wearing.

"I didn't mean it like that," Steph said, easing up the zipper. "You all right? Is this just bridal nerves or are you coming down with something? Want me to call Larry?"

"No, I don't want you to call the new family doctor," she said.

"Are you upset because I didn't want to go along with Gillian's offer to throw us a double wedding? You know how I've always dreamed of a June wedding and—"

Charity rubbed her forehead. "I'd have been happy either way. Have your June wedding. I promise I'm fine with it."

"Good," Steph said. "And here I've been worried all afternoon that I was the cause of your funk."

"Quit it," Charity said, yanking off the dress. "I

wish everyone would stop asking what's wrong. In less than eight weeks I'm marrying a guy I've loved forever. What in the world could possibly be wrong with that?"

"Nothing," Steph said, holding out the next dress—an antebellum number with a skirt wider than Charity was tall. "Which is why I don't understand why you're being so hard to please. If you're to have any chance at having a dress altered in time for the wedding, you're going to have to pick one today."

"All right," Charity said. "I will. Just quit nagging me—about everything."

CHARITY RETURNED HOME exhausted only to upon opening the door get the most energizing vision of her life.

"Bug," Adam complained, "Gillian promised she'd have you out at least another hour." He looked beyond-words gorgeous on her sofa, wearing nothing but jeans and a suspicious grin as he tossed one of her only two good towels over something on the coffee table.

"Want me to leave?" she asked, only just now re-alizing that the man and the wedding were really, truly happening.

Tears filled her eyes and she shut the door, then ran to Adam, all but throwing herself into his arms.

"Hey," he crooned, smoothing her hair. "What's wrong? Brides aren't supposed to be weepy."

"I—I know," she said. "It's just that you've backed out on me so many times that—"

"To be fair, I've only backed out on an official proposal once." He kissed her forehead and cheeks, then pulled her onto his lap, gently rocking while she clung to him tighter still. "Trust me, my buglicious beauty, from here on out, I'm going nowhere."

She nodded, swallowed hard.

"Now, tell me, did you find a dress?"

"N-no," she said through lingering sniffles. "But Gregory said he'd find a few more to show me tomorrow afternoon."

"Need another day off? Franks would probably give you one."

"No," she said, sliding off of Adam and onto her feet in search of tissue. "Probably what I need is to get back to work."

"We'll be glad to have you." He got up, too, wandering into the kitchen to grab a beer from the fridge. He popped the top and took a sip, standing there in her kitchen, bare-chested, scratching his abs.

To most women, this might not have been such a significant thing—a guy standing in her kitchen downing a beer and scratching. But to her, having loved him as long as Charity had, she felt a new batch of tears over the fact that he was finally, really and truly, on the verge of being forever hers.

Out of that knowledge came the confidence that she had what it took to be a great mom. And a great marshal.

No more worries. All she had to do now was to revel in what would surely be the happiest time of her life.

Shyly smiling, she walked right up to him, planting her hands squarely on his chest. It was high time she put all this second-guessing behind her and take this engagement out for a test drive. "Is it time for bed?" she asked.

"Sleepy?" He hooked his free arm around her waist, pulling her in for another kiss on the top of her head when where she most keenly craved his lips was on a bit lower spot.

"Not particularly."

Pushing her back, a devilish grin lighting his eyes, he said, "You aren't propositioning me, are you?"

"Maybe."

"Hot damn." He parked his beer on the counter, then swooped her into his arms "By all means, let's go straight to bed."

WHEN CHARITY'S ALARM went off Tuesday morning, and Adam was there in her bed, one arm around her, the other swatting the incessant beep, she knew everything would be all right. Even while he'd made love to her, she'd had this irrational fear that in the morning he'd be gone. As though the past twenty-four hours had just been a dream.

"Morning, beautiful," he said with that slow, sexy grin she so loved.

"Morning."

"If we shared a shower, think we could be good?"

"We were *good* last night."

He feigned shock. "Cracking dirty jokes before you've even had your morning coffee? I'm marrying a wicked woman—and I like her…" He growled, tackling her with a few playful nips and kisses. "A lot."

Charity hadn't known a shower could be such fun. And when Adam demanded she eat her breakfast in bed, she wasn't about to turn him down.

"I could get used to this pampering," she said, forkful of cheesy scrambled eggs to her mouth.

"Good. Because for what I've put you through, you've got the rest of your life still to go."

Thirty minutes later, eggs churning, Charity surrendered her car keys to Adam and he drove them to work.

"You know," she said, exhausted from just their hike from the garage to their office. "I think the true reason you proposed is because you like driving my car."

He clutched his chest. "You got me."

She slugged him, then, when he whined she hit too hard, she kissed not only the supposed sore spot, but his lips.

"Come on, guys," Bear said in passing. "Get a room."

Charity giggled.

"Did you find it?" Bear asked, walking alongside her since having nudged Adam out of the way.

"What?" she asked.

"Your wedding dress. Duh."

"Oops." Casting a wink over her shoulder, she said, "Guess I'm still dazed by a certain someone's kisses."

"Oh, puke," Bear said, holding open the office door.

Charity's bliss continued for the next hour or so, at least until Franks called the lot of them into his office. On his desk sat an awesome-smelling bag of microwaved popcorn. Adam's eggs had been good, but popcorn sounded like a fantastic breakfast. Was it too soon to eat again?

"Listen up," he said once they'd all taken seats. "I know last week's protective gig was unorthodox, but it got the job done."

Charity grinned while Beau put his arm around her and squeezed. Everyone else in the room—aside from Sam—shared a laugh.

"All fun aside, we have a real situation brewing in Freeporte. Judge William Morningside is hearing a drug case, and last night, 'round about 2:00 a.m., the defendant's posse stormed the county jail. Killed four guards in the process. Good family men. Our star dealer, Sanchez, and four of his playmates got away. Local authorities caught three. Sanchez, however, is still at large, spreading sunshine in the form of notes. When Judge Morningside arrived at his gym this morning, this was taped to his locker." Franks passed copies of a crudely written note to all assembled. It read:

Drop all charges against Jose Luis Sanchez or we'll drop your wife off Boseman's Bridge.

"A few years back," Adam said, "I bungeed off that bridge. You wouldn't wanna go over without a rope. It spans a hellacious gorge."

Charity fought a fresh wave of nausea just thinking about it. Maybe she'd skip the popcorn.

"Seriously, gang, this is the real deal. Caleb, you're in charge. Have a team in place by eleven hundred hours. Questions?" When none were asked, he said, "Good. Let's get busy."

Once everyone, save for Charity, had filed out of Franks's office, Adam asked the boss, "Sir, there any chance of Charity sticking back here? You know, finishing up paperwork and what-not till we get this creep behind bars?"

"Excuse me?" Charity said. "I happen to be standing right beside you. And, no, I don't want to stay behind, stuck with paperwork, while you guys are off having all the fun." Yes, she very much wanted to have a baby and at least scale down her workload until the kid was in school, but that didn't mean she was ready to be put out to pasture!

Franks sighed. "No one could be happier about the two of you getting hitched than myself," he said. "But, dammit, Logue, your wife-to-be is one of my best men—so to speak. If I have to hear this chauvinistic, overbearing, overprotective crap every time I assign you two to a mission, one of you is for sure staying home—and believe me, it won't be your wife. Got it?"

"Yessir," Adam said.

"Good. In the future, you'll be assigned to work different divisions, but for now, I don't have the manpower for that luxury. Now, get out of here and assemble your gear. Oh—and send Caleb back in. I want to make it clear, Adam, he knows you're to be on your best behavior."

"But, sir—"

"Logue…" the boss warned.

"Yessir. I'll send Caleb right in."

"Can you believe that?" Adam asked in the hall, Franks's office door closed behind him. "What a prick."

"Yeah, you are," Charity said. "I can't believe you pulled that stunt back there. What were you thinking?"

"Is it wrong of me to want to keep you safe?"

"If it comes at the expense of a career I've worked hard at, and happen to also be damned good at."

He rolled his eyes. "Your job at the moment is planning our wedding. You'll no doubt be distracted, worrying about frosting flavors and flowers and stuff. What if you're trying to decide if you like…I don't know, petunias or daisies better when someone pulls a gun? Your reaction time'll be off and then whammo, blammo. My bride's dead before I even slip my ring on her finger."

"Because I love you," Charity said, fury bubbling up her throat in the form of cheesy-egg bile. "I'm going to pretend you took a strong medication of some sort this morning that currently has you *waaaay* off-kilter."

"Pretend all you want," he said. "But I love you,

too, and if something happened to you on my watch, I'd—"

"What? Never forgive yourself? Adam, I've been watching out for myself a whole thirty-five years without your help. Sweetie, I think I can manage a few more before retirement."

"I know," he said, pulling her into a fierce hug. "And I'm sorry for worrying, but from the second Franks told us about this Sanchez threatening not the judge, but his wife, I can only focus on my future wife."

Grinning, standing on her tiptoes to kiss the tip of his nose, Charity said, "Fortunately for you, your bride is quite adept at kicking ass. Now, let's stock up on ammo and go grab ourselves a bad guy."

Chapter Thirteen

Adam hated to admit it, but with Charity, Bear, Caleb and Sam watching the judge's wife while he and Beau stuck close to the judge, he felt as if he was only doing half his job. He was so freaked over Charity possibly being in harm's way, he couldn't even think straight. Lord help him if he had to shoot straight.

What was wrong with him? Ever since proposing to Charity, then having her accept, he was happy— over the moon, thrilled—but he was also on edge. Once she became his—and yes, he knew it was chauvinistic to think of marriage in those terms, but he didn't care—he'd take his vows seriously. Especially the protection part. Charity meant the world to him and if he had to move the world to keep her safe, that was what he'd damn well do.

"Ready to roll?" Beau asked in Adam's earpiece from across the courtroom, eyeing Judge Morningside, who was getting ready to leave his bench.

Escorting the judge to his chambers was a brief trip. In under a minute the short, balding man was safely inside, munching on a pepperoni pizza his wife had had delivered.

"Any news from Caleb's team?" Adam asked his brother.

"No," Beau said with a big sigh. "And for the fifteenth time, she's safe with Caleb. He'll watch after Charity like he would either of us."

"Yeah, well, I want him watching her better than that."

"Give it a rest, would you?" Beau shook his head. "I thought once you two jumped each other's bones you'd loosen up, but if anything, sleeping with Charity has only made you more of a pain in my ass."

"Nice talk," Adam said. "I appreciate all this brotherly love."

"You're welcome," Beau said with the kind of glare he'd used back when Adam got a peanut butter and grape sandwich stuck in Beau's bike chain. "Now get your head off of your fiancée and back on the judge."

"MIGHT NOT BE so bad being a judge's wife," Charity mused as the team trailed her from a posh salon where she'd gotten her nails and hair done, to a posh boutique where she shopped for a cocktail dress to wear to Congresswoman Valencia's electoral watch party. The two had been sorority sisters at Oregon

State, and if Valencia won her reelection bid, Cookie, the nickname everyone called the judge's wife, had been promised the job of decorating her friend's Washington, D.C. office and apartment.

Charity had learned all of this while guarding Cookie's dressing room.

"What do you think of this one?" Cookie asked, examining her backside in the three-way mirror at the far end of the sumptuous, cream-colored dressing area.

"Gorgeous," Charity said. "The mossy-green looks amazing with your red hair."

"Thanks. I've always wanted to wear brighter tones, but they never seem to work."

"Seeing how pretty you look in what you have on," Charity said, "I wouldn't worry about it."

"You're a doll." The middle-aged woman stepped back into her cube. "You don't really think I'm in danger, do you? I just assumed that boy's note was trash talk."

"Hard to say, ma'am."

"Please," she said, poking her head out the door. "Call me Cookie. Everyone does."

"Thanks," Charity said.

"So back on topic, deep down, do you honestly think this Sanchez man is out to hurt either me or my husband?"

"I'd like to hope not," Charity said. "But I've been a marshal for over a decade, and in that time have seen a lot of twisted things. Don't get me wrong, I'm not trying to scare you or to imply your case is any more dangerous than others I've been assigned to. Just that it never hurts to be cautious."

"Hmm…" Cookie said, eyeing herself in the next dress—a slinky cranberry-colored number. "Speaking of caution, is this too racy for a woman my age?"

"You're only as young as you feel is what I always say, and if you feel half as great as you look, you just found a winner."

Cookie laughed. "I like you," she said. "We're going to get along just fine."

Her own smile fading, Charity said, "I only wish I'd had such an easy time wedding-dress shopping."

"You're getting married? When?"

"Christmas."

"Fantastic," Cookie said, suddenly excited. "You'll make a gorgeous holiday bride."

If only Charity had as much confidence!

"HOW'D YOUR DAY GO?" Adam asked, back at the motel. Per Franks's request, he was officially bunking with Beau, but he had taken the liberty of stopping by Charity's for a visit.

"Nice," she said, washing her face at the plain-Jane room's counter sink. Whoever occupied the room next door had some obnoxious cops-and-robber show on their TV. Between dorky, seventies-style chase music and gunshots, he had to reposition himself from the head of the bed to the foot just to hear her. "Cookie Morningside's a doll. I hope she doesn't get hurt."

"She's got a great security team," Adam said, bunching a pillow under his head.

"Yeah, I know." She winked.

"Sorry about this morning," he said a few minutes later. "I was out of line."

"True."

"It won't happen again."

"I know that, too." While she grinned, he leaned forward to swat her behind. "Mmm…a spankin'. The perfect end to any working girl's day."

He scrambled to his feet, walked up behind her and slid his hands around her waist. "Do you wake each day planning ways to tick me off?"

"Pretty much." She grinned at him in the mirror.

"All kidding aside," he said, catching her stare. "I know I was a bad boy. Beau read me the riot act, and as a bonus prize, my dad even called, telling me not to ruin a good thing."

"That good thing…" she teased. "Would that be me?"

"You know it." He kissed her ear.

Giggling, she scrunched her neck. "Is it time for bed?"

"Sleepy?"

"Not particularly."

He groaned before sweeping her into his arms. "How did you know those were exactly the words I was wanting to hear?"

"I JUST CAN'T DECIDE," Cookie said the next morning. "Should I go wild and have the shoes and purse dyed to match the cranberry or just wear black?"

"If it were me," Charity said, eyeing the beautiful silk-and-sequin dress Cookie had tried on the day before, "and money wasn't an issue, I'd have them dyed."

"Great, let's do it." She left the closet that was larger than Charity's living room. "Oh, and I'll have to ask William's mother if I might borrow her diamond necklace and earring set. Oh, Charity, wait till you see them. They're divine." On her way to her dressing table, an elegant skirted affair larger than Charity's kitchen table, she said, "Family rumor has it that they were given to Mother Morningside by a man other than Father Morningside. He used to get all bent out of shape when she wore them—mostly on special occasions, but sometimes just to one of our son's football games. I swear she did it just to annoy her husband."

Laughing, Charity said, "This is a woman I'd love to meet."

"You'll get a chance Saturday night—if you're still here. Every Saturday night, we supper at the club. Even if you all have caught that dreadful

Sanchez man by then, I want you and Adam to join us. William speaks very highly of your fiancé." The previous afternoon, Cookie had pressed her for not just wedding, but groom details.

"It's a date," Charity said, squeezing the woman in a spontaneous hug. How they'd gotten so close in such a short time, Charity couldn't figure. Maybe it was because Cookie had admitted to always having wanted a daughter, and she was already up to her neck in helping Gillian with her ever-growing wedding plans.

"All right then," Cookie said with bright smile. "Now that that's settled, let's hop in the car and get a fabric swatch over to—"

A crash was followed by breaking glass.

"Get down!" Charity hollered, throwing herself over Cookie, dragging her off of the cushioned bench and onto the carpeted floor. Into the microphone tucked up her sleeve, she said, "I need backup in the master suite. Possible intrusion attempt and—"

Before she'd even finished her request, Caleb was there, quickly followed by Sam and Bear.

"Keep her down," Caleb directed.

Cookie was crying, and though Charity's heart went out to her, she did as she was told and kept her in what had to be an uncomfortable position.

Bear knelt to pick up a rock. A red rubber band held what appeared to be a note.

"Got gloves?" Caleb asked.

"Yeah," Bear said.

"Use 'em. I want this done by the book. Sam, everything look all clear out the window?"

"Affirmative."

"Charity—get Mrs. Morningside out of here and into an interior room. Bear, soon as you get those gloves on, get me a read on that note."

Charity rose, giving Cookie the freedom to get to her feet, but still covering her back.

Bear read, "'Drop all charges or Cookie crumbles.'"

The judge's wife shrieked. "Oh, my God. This isn't happening. Please tell me this isn't—"

"Charity," Caleb barked. "Get her out of here—now."

"Come on," Charity said, urging Cookie along. "Everything's going to be all right."

"But my husband. Where's William?"

Caleb said, "He's safe and sound at the courthouse, ma'am. Don't you worry about a thing. He's in good hands."

In a small media room, Charity got Cookie settled into a comfy burgundy lounge chair. "How about watching a movie?" she asked.

"Oh, dear, no. I couldn't possibly. Not with all this intrigue hanging over my head."

"I know this has got to be frightening for you," Charity said, patting the older woman's hand. "But I don't know any better medicine than a nice, romantic comedy."

"Well…I do like *Pretty Woman* an awful lot. Think you could put that on?"

"Sure. Richard Gere is highly medicinal."

"Oh, dear…"

"What's wrong?" Charity asked, forehead furrowed with concern.

"My shoes. If we don't get them today, how will they ever be dyed in time?"

"That is a problem," Charity said. "How about if I make a few calls and see if the shoe store might be willing to come to us?"

"You're such a dear," Cookie said. "How will I ever thank you?"

"Just a have a super time at your friend's party."

After insuring her charge was engrossed in the movie, Charity slipped out into the hall and closed the door. She found Bear in the bedroom, while the rest of team were at their security posts.

"Any new developments?" she asked.

"Not a thing," Bear said. "This guy's a ghost. We're still not sure how he made it past the front gates of the development." He sighed, rubbed his forehead. "Cookie all right?"

"She will be as long as I get in touch with her favorite shoe salesman."

"Huh?"

"Long story," Charity said. "It's a chick thing. I've gotta make a quick call, then will be posted outside the media room."

WITH THE INCREASED threat on Cookie came increased protection, meaning none of the double shifts that typically came along with small-scale jobs. As a result, Charity was back at the motel by six.

She entered her room to find the TV blaring and three sacks of wonderful-smelling barbecue takeout scattered across the small table in front of the beige room's only window.

Adam, in all his male glory, sauntered out of the bathroom wearing unbuttoned jeans and a smile. His chest hair and the rummaged-through mess on his head were damp. "'Bout time you got home."

"Mmm..." she said, closing the door on her hectic day and stepping into the outstretched arms of the man who would hopefully give her an idyllic night. "Are you ever a sight for sore eyes."

"Rough day?" he asked.

"Nah." She stepped back and around him, reaching into the overnight case she'd stashed on top of the dresser and had yet to unpack. "Just long—and boring. Really, *really* boring."

Grabbing black cropped sweatpants and one of the new T-shirts her sister had made her buy two sizes smaller than Charity normally wore, she said, "S'cuze me. I need a quick shower."

"Want me to join you?"

More than anything Charity wanted to say yes, but she was still shaken up about Cookie's close call. She hardly knew the woman, yet felt strangely connected to her. In an hour or two, she'd be decompressed, but at this moment, in an intimate setting like the shower, one kiss and hug, and she'd break. Better for Adam's overactive imagination that he assumed all was still calm.

"Well?" he asked, strumming his fingers down her cheek. "Is that a yes or no?"

"Ordinarily, you know I'd love it, but…"

"Jeez Louise," he said with a smile to match his teasing tone. "We're not even married yet and already you're putting the kibosh on my fun."

"Adam, I—"

"Shh." He planted a kiss to her forehead. "I know. I'm a hot water hog, and for once, you're wanting it all to yourself. Go on. I'll get dinner set up."

"Thanks for the meal," she said on her way into the still-steamy bathroom. "And for understanding."

"That's me. Mr. Understanding."

After she shut the door, a muscle started popping on Adam's tightly clenched jaw.

What was she trying to pull, hiding the afternoon's events? Did she think he was dumb and wouldn't find out?

If he were one of his brothers, he could be calm. Overlook what to her had probably been a case of trying not to make him worry. But dammit, he couldn't help the fact that he had a short fuse any more than he could help that now that he was marrying Bug, he existed in a state of 24/7 worry for her safety.

Slamming open the bathroom door, he pulled back the flimsy white vinyl curtain and stepped in, jeans and all.

"Adam!" Bug shrieked.

"Why did you lie to me?"

"W-what are you doing? You're still dressed."

"Why did you lie?"

"I—I didn't."

God help him but she was beautiful, hands over her head, rinsing shampoo from her hair, suds cascading over full breasts and her taut belly.

"Dammit, Bug." Despite her glory, he couldn't get past her having chosen to build the foundation of their marriage on a bald-faced lie. "I know what went down this afternoon with Mrs. Morningside. I know the rock came damned close to hitting your head, and that you, always being closest to the woman, are in the eye of the storm should our guy decide to give up rocks in favor of bullets."

She'd brought her hands down and crossed her arms, covering her breasts, but not the steely edged will in her eyes. "For your information, in not telling you, I was trying to protect you. And I didn't lie. Just omitted select information."

"You told me your afternoon was boring."

"Okay, so maybe I told you a little lie, but, Adam, it was for your own good. Look how you reacted when we were first assigned to this case. You went nuts—asking Franks to switch me over to a nice, safe, dull desk job. I went through the same training as you, and I scored way higher than you in marksmanship, so—"

"Not way higher," he argued.

"Oh, brother," she said, throwing her hands up only to slap them against her thighs. "You're psycho. And I just signed up for a lifetime of this?"

"Hey, darlin', you claimed to love me. And this is me at my finest. Sorry, but I care if you get hurt."

"And what? You think I don't? You think I want to get myself shot and miss a wedding I've looked forward to starring in for what feels like my whole life?"

"That's just it." His voice thundered. "I don't know what to think." Softening, he pulled her hard against him, crushing her in a hug. "I love you. I've been a fool for not seeing it sooner. But I love you, I love—"

"Stop," she said, fingers over his mouth, then lips. "I love you, too. I'm sorry for lying, I just—"

"No, I'm sorry. Yet again, I went off half-cocked."

"No, I should've been straight with you."

"You're wet," he said with a laugh.

"So are you," she said with a giggle. "And you have far too many clothes on."

"Just jeans."

"Sorry, Mr. Logue, but the jeans will have to come off."

Chapter Fourteen

"This was really sweet," Charity said an hour later, after they'd finally dried off. "I didn't realize how hungry I was until finding this delicious spread."

"Sorry it's cold," he said, not looking the least bit remorseful.

"Right. And I'll be dying my hair purple for our upcoming nuptials."

"I think the lobby has a microwave for those pseudo breakfasts they serve. Want me to haul at least the meat down there and nuke it?"

"Nah…" She winked. "Let's just hurry up and eat. Then we can get back to—" Leaning across the table, she whispered her naughty idea in his ear.

"Damn, woman," he said, shoveling slaw onto her plate. "Had I known we had that to look forward to for dessert, I'd have served you dinner when you first walked in the door."

AFTER AN HOUR on the job Thursday morning, Adam hid a yawn behind his sleeve. Hot damn, what a night. He was a fool for having missed out on Charity's hidden talents all these years.

Warmed by memories of last night, Adam could almost feel himself drifting off when he heard Beau's voice in his ear. "Yo, bro? You awake over there?"

"Yeah, why?" Adam asked, using the mike hidden up his suit sleeve.

"There was trouble at the judge's house."

Adam's heart thundered. "And..."

"Adam, I want you to stay calm, but—"

"Dammit, Beau," he stormed into his mike, ignoring the bailiff's glare. "Tell me what happened."

"All you need know is that Charity went down, but now, she's fine. Caleb also asked me to pass along the fact that if you for one second think of leaving your post, Franks is gonna fire your ass faster than—"

Too late, Beau thought, watching his hotheaded brother leave the courtroom. Though professionally, Beau knew Adam was playing Russian roulette, Beau had to admit, even if it was only to himself, that had their roles been reversed, and Gracie was the one who'd been shot, a team of ten marshals couldn't have kept him from being with her.

Godspeed, little bro.

"Hey," Charity said, gazing up from her hospital bed to see her hunky man. "I thought you were supposed to be in court?"

"I was. But I'd rather be with you."

"How'd you get Beau to let you go?" she asked. "Until Sanchez is caught, I thought Franks was adamant about having full teams on both the judge and Cookie at all times?"

"Beau found a sub for me. My brother's a great guy, huh?"

"I'll say." Charity reached for Adam's hand. "I'll have to be sure and thank him."

"Nah," Adam said, releasing her hand to fiddle with a purple iris in the massive flower basket Cookie and the Judge had sent. Was it the flowers' rich scent making him sick, or his deception? "Beau's funny about that kind of thing. Doesn't like to be fawned over for doing acts of kindness. Says it makes him feel girly."

Charity wrinkled her nose. "Are you making that up?"

"Come on," he said with a laugh. "I'm not that creative."

"Good point." She joined in on his laughter. "All right, I promise my lips are sealed, even though I'm thrilled you're here."

"In a lot of pain?" he asked, pulling up a chair to sit beside her.

"No. The bullet just grazed my leg. In fact, the only reason I'm stuck in this bed is because of a surprise the doctor discovered."

His expression darkened. "You don't have cancer, or something, do you?"

"Adam!" She playfully smacked him. "Would you

for once quit thinking the worst and try coming up with the most amazing reason in the world you could think of for me being held over."

"You're in the hospital," he said, leaning forward, brushing stray hair from her forehead. "Nothing good comes out of hospitals except—no way." He raised his eyebrows. "You're pregnant?"

Nodding, tearing just like she had when the doctor had first told her, she gushed, "Can you believe it? Adam, sweetie, we're going to have a baby."

He stood, pulling her into an awkward hug, only to abruptly release her. "I didn't hurt you, did I?"

"No. I'm pregnant, not broken."

"Still, you must have something wrong with you, or—"

"The doctor wants to keep me overnight for observation. I lost some blood and was a little woozier than most folks. The doc asked if there was a chance I could be pregnant. I told him there was, but just microscopic. He tested me anyway and voilà."

Adam curved his big hands over her still-flat stomach. Hard to believe there was a kid inside. *His* kid! "This is blow-my-mind amazing. Have I told you lately how much I love you?" he asked.

"I love you, too," she said. "We're going to have a great life."

"I'm just asking, so don't get upset, but are you going to go on maternity leave?"

"Now?"

"Yeah. I mean, you've just been shot. Don't you think you should lay low for a while? Just laze around, take it easy?"

"Sure," she said, cupping her hand to his cheek, searching his eyes. "I'll do all of that in about eight months when I'll be rolling after bad guys instead of running."

"Okay," he said. "Whatever you say."

"You're not going to fight me?" she asked, scarcely believing this was the same man who'd fought their boss over her being assigned to this case.

He shrugged. "If you want to work, you want to work. Not much I can, or should say about it. I'm starting a new leaf, remember?"

"Of course, I remember," she said. "I'm just shocked—and impressed you do."

"Anything for you, angel." He leaned over the bed rail to kiss her belly. "And you."

"WHAT DO YOU MEAN, you want me to pack up and go back to Portland?" Adam asked Caleb at eight that night over coffee and snacks in the hospital cafeteria. This time of night, the place was deserted save for a few teens playing cards at a back table. Their laughter felt out of place.

"Just what I said." His brother was stone-faced.

"Oh, I get it." Adam grinned while setting down his dry roast beef sandwich. "Charity put you up to this, didn't she?"

"No, bud. Sorry, but this is the real deal. Straight from Franks. Effective immediately, you're temporarily relieved of your duties. Six weeks unpaid vacation for leaving your post."

"What the—?" Adam shook his head.

"By his own admission, Franks said he's being overly harsh, but he wants you to learn a lesson you'll never forget. Especially once you and Charity tie the knot."

"Beau knew where I was headed. She'd just been shot! Can you honestly tell me if Allie was hurt, you wouldn't want to see her ASAP?"

"We're not talking about Allie, but Charity who, granted, is your fiancée, but technically, as far as this case is concerned, she should mean no more to you than a fellow marshal. You abandoned a man you were sworn to protect."

"Oh, come on," Adam said, shoving his plate halfway across the table. "It's the judge's wife our guy wants to off. Beau was in that courtroom along with four other guys. They didn't even need me. Judge Morningside was safe as—"

"You're not going to fast-talk your way out of this. Hand me your star and piece."

"What?" Lurching back, Adam said, "The hell I'm giving you my star. I worked hard for that thing."

His brother held out his hand. *"Now."*

"But—"

Caleb just sat there, stone-faced, with his palm out.

Head spinning, stomach sick, Adam handed over the star that had been the only thing keeping him sane after Angela's death. The job used to be everything to him. Aside from Charity, it still was. And, hell, he never would've left the judge had he believed for one second the guy had been in danger. All tucked into his courtroom, he'd been safe as a baby in his momma's arms.

"Your gun, too," Caleb said.

Adam released his clip, then reluctantly handed it and the weapon over. "You're a shit to be doing this to your own family."

"Right back atcha," Caleb said without an ounce of remorse or compassion. "I can't believe you were stupid enough to have landed me in this position."

"Yeah, well, Dad's gonna kick your ass when—"

"Get out of here, Adam. And don't show up at the Portland office until you're invited back."

"But what am I going to tell Charity? I'm on probation with her, man. If she finds out about this, she's not going to understand."

"Damn straight. Because she's good at her job. She follows the rules."

"Okay, so I screwed up. Again. But, please, don't tell her about this. Let it be our little secret."

"*Little* secret? Adam, you're weeks from marrying the woman. Don't you think she deserves to know the truth? She told me how you went off on her for not telling you straight out about the rock-through-the-window incident."

"That was the *old* me," Adam said, mouth dry, pulse surging. He had to get Caleb to see this from his point of view. "Now that there's a baby on the way, I'm officially turning a new leaf."

"Charity's pregnant?"

"Uh-huh. I'm good, huh?" Adam winked.

Caleb groaned. "That's wonderful, man. I'm truly happy for you."

"So you'll keep this whole unpaid leave thing just between us?"

He sighed, glanced off toward the bored blonde manning the cafeteria checkout counter. Even from twenty feet away, Adam heard her drumming her long, fake nails on the stainless-steel counter.

"Please," Adam begged. "With the wedding and baby and all, Charity has enough on her plate without having to worry about me. I promise I'll use this time to get my act together."

Caleb said, "I'm as big a fool for going along with this as you were for running out of that court-room, but what can I say? I'm a sucker for love, and I love Charity. The last thing I want is for anything to bring her down. This is supposed to be a happy, fun time for her, and she shouldn't have the days leading up to her wedding brought down by the likes of you."

"BUT WHY?" Charity asked Adam, sitting cross-legged in her hospital bed. Down the hall, someone's monitor kept going off and the beeping was driving her crazy. So was their boss's ridiculous decision.

"Shouldn't you be flat, or something?" Adam asked, gesturing to her awkward position.

Trying to be amenable, she straightened one leg. "Seriously, Adam, why is Franks reassigning you? We're a team. We should stick together."

"I know," he said. "But probably this isn't such a bad thing. It's really sort of a promotion. The boss said he's putting me on a top-secret witness protection thing."

"But you'll be in Portland the whole time?"

"Yep."

"Who are you protecting? I don't recall anything big coming down the pipe."

"It's sudden," he said. "Super hush-hush."

"But what about the wedding?" she asked. From the dispenser on the bedside table, she pulled a tissue, then blew her nose. With a fresh tissue, she blotted teary eyes. "We're already short on time. Are you going to be able to help with the planning?"

"Absolutely," he said. "I'll just be a phone call away."

"So I won't ever get to see you?" That devastating thought had her reaching for still more tissues.

"Well, maybe once or twice I'll manage to sneak away, but I promise to call every day."

When she pouted, he climbed into bed with her

and her mountain of used tissue, tugging her onto his lap. "I'll miss you," she said.

"Ditto," he said, thoroughly kissing her. "You be safe."

Crying, nodding, she said, "You, too."

"No tears." With the pads of his thumbs, he dried her cheeks. "Before you know it, this'll be over and everything'll be back to normal. Only better. 'Cause you'll be my wife, and I'll be your husband and we can go baby shopping and—" He kissed her again, this time hard, with a spooky intensity.

"Adam?" she asked when he paused for air.

"Uh-huh?"

"Is everything all right?" Her neighbor's beeping monitor finally stopped. The sudden quiet was deafening.

"How do you mean?"

"You did tell me *everything?* I mean, this isn't like some crazy, kamikaze mission you're going on, is it?"

"No way," he promised. "I'm about to be a dad. From here on out, I'm playing it safe, and I'll expect you to do the same."

SATURDAY, CHARITY FOUND herself complying to Adam's safety expectations whether she'd wanted to or not. Sanchez had been taken out in a surprisingly dull twist of fate that'd led marshals who'd been trailing him to catch him while doing his laundry at the Suds & Soak.

Just as well, seeing how once Cookie heard through the grapevine of Charity's pregnancy, she'd politely demanded she be taken off of her case. Not because she'd thought Charity would no longer do good work, but because she wanted her to be safe. Unfortunately, Franks agreed, meaning she was on paperwork duty for the next eight months.

That fact didn't bring her down near as much as being without Adam. She hadn't realized just how much time they spent together until being forced to be without him. True to his word, though, he'd called both nights he'd been gone, never giving her specifics on his case, but at least letting her know he was safe and cared.

Even though she was without a date, Cookie had wanted Charity to join her and the judge and his mother for their promised dinner date, but Charity had politely declined. She was tired. Bone-deep, achy tired that she suspected had more to do with Adam's absence than the baby.

One week came, and then another, until it was Thanksgiving, and Charity found herself feeling alone amongst a sea of soon-to-be family and friends. Steph was celebrating with Dr. Larry, and while Gillian and Joe had offered to fly her folks in for the occasion, they'd turned her down since they couldn't find anyone to watch the farm animals for them while they'd be gone. Now that her father was retired, they'd turned their country home into what for all practical purposes might as well be a petting zoo. Her mother had relayed that her father had already hired a man for Christmas, but for Thanksgiving, they hadn't had much luck finding an extra hand. Leaving Charity on her own with all of the Logues as well as Joe's former in-laws and Allie's mom—currently flirting up a storm with Adam's dad.

"More dressing?" Gillian asked, hovering beside Charity with a heaping spoon.

"No, thanks," Charity said, wondering how she could be glum in such outrageously opulent surroundings. Gillian's dining room was a replica of a stone-walled Medieval dining hall they'd toured while on a trip to Scotland. The wooden cathedral ceiling had to be at least twenty-five feet high. Age-old, wall-hung tapestries provided much-needed warmth, as well as a massive stone hearth occupying nearly the whole south wall—inside of which a fire merrily crackled. The table was a sturdy oak affair, long enough for thirty. Soft classical music flowed from hidden speakers.

"You should eat more," Gillian argued, putting a roll on Charity's plate. "You've hardly put on any weight. If you're worried about your dress fitting, don't. I've found you the best tailor money can buy. He's promised to make your dress look stunning regardless of the state of your tummy." She patted Charity's stomach. "Hello in there."

"Relax." Grinning, Charity said, "I won't even be showing for another couple months."

"All the same, if you're worried—about any-thing—don't."

While everyone else talked sports over the turkey and ham and at least a dozen side dishes Gracie and a team of chefs had prepared, Charity sat angled on her seat, facing her future sister-in-law and for the first time since Adam had left, revealing how ill at ease she was with Adam's supposedly top-secret as-signment. "I'm a fellow agent, Gillian, but it's the oddest thing. Men I've worked with for years won't make eye contact with me. In fact, most everyone at the office just avoids me. I've never felt so ostracized. And I don't have the foggiest idea why. It's like I've got some dread disease."

"You know men." Gillian clucked. "They're prob-ably not sure what to make of the wedding plans and all. You've gone from being one of the guys to a bride. Maybe they're feeling—"

"This a private party?" Adam asked at the room's oversize door. "Or do you all let in bums off the street?"

"Adam!" Charity scraped her chair back, practi-cally knocking him down with a running jump. Tossing her arms around his neck and legs around his hips, she said, "I've missed you so bad."

"Same here," he said into her hair, face buried in the crook of her neck. "Lord, you smell great."

"You, too. Are you home for good?"

"Not just yet, but I'm hoping soon."

"Can you at least tell me where you've been?"

"Sorry," he said, setting her to her feet. "The whole thing's pretty covert."

"Sure," she said, trying not to pout. "I understand."

"Thanks." He slipped his arm around her waist. "Having your support makes this easier."

"What's that?" Caleb asked.

"You know," Adam said, pressing a kiss to the top of Charity's head.

"Sure, but does everyone else? Dad," Caleb asked their father. "Do you have any idea what Adam, here, has been up to?"

"This is not the time," Vince said, his voice and expression resolute.

Was Charity only imagining it, or was there tension between her fiancé and his brother?

"Oh, sure," Caleb said, a touch of sarcasm in his tone. "How could I forget? A secret as important as yours shouldn't be talked about in family circles."

Charity caught Adam passing Caleb a dirty look, but he didn't say a word, just sat at the fresh place setting Gillian had laid for him, then grabbed hold of Charity's hand. What would account for Caleb's nasty attitude? Was he jealous that Adam had leap-frogged ahead of him for this apparently prestigious assignment?

Everyone around the office knew once Franks retired, Caleb would most likely be promoted to Oregon's next presidentially appointed U.S. Marshal. Was all this tension a case of sibling rivalry?

"Gillian," Adam said, helping himself to turkey, "this is an amazing spread you've got here."

"Thanks," Gillian said, "but all I did was plan the floral arrangements. Gracie handled the cooking."

"Well, Gracie," Adam said with a generous smile, "you've outdone yourself. Everything looks—and I'm sure, tastes—delicious."

Gracie frowned. "I'm pleased with everything but the mashed potatoes. They're Beau's favorite, so I tried making a bigger batch than usual. They're off. But I can't quite figure out what's missing."

"So you blame it on me?" Beau asked.

"You're the most convenient one," Gracie teased her husband.

Meggie piped in with, "I think the taters are good, Aunt Gracie!"

"Me, too," added Caleb Jr.

"Uh-huh," said Gillian and Joe's daughter, Chrissy.

With it unanimously decided the potatoes were delicious and Gracie was too hard on her own cooking, the tension eased between Adam and Caleb and conversation wound around to the usual family chatter on upcoming vacation and holiday plans— only this time those plans happened to coincide with Charity and Adam's Christmas wedding and Paris honeymoon that it'd been decided the whole family would be going on. Seeing how Joe and Gillian had rented a chateau just outside the city, the newlyweds would have their own private wing.

With Adam beside her, for Charity, at least, the day took on a surreal happy glow. It was hard to believe how perfectly everything had turned out between them.

From dinner, they all joined in to wash dishes, then settled into the massive theater room to watch football on the roll-down TV screen that made Judge Morningside's plenty-big flat screen look like a toy.

"Are you spending the night?" Charity whisper-asked Adam around nine, when all the games had gone off and the few of them not splashing in the indoor pool were in the midst of a James Bond film fest.

"I'd love to," he said, "but I really should get back."

"Please, Adam," she begged, palm against his chest. "I've missed you so bad. Phone calls just aren't the same as waking up beside you." She proved how much she'd missed him with a heated kiss.

"Let me call Franks," he said, apparently as revved up as she was. "Seeing how it's a holiday, I bet he'll give me the night off."

"I'll just bet he will," Caleb said wryly from the row of reclining seats in front of them.

Chapter Fifteen

That's it. It might not be any of Charity's business, but she'd had enough of Caleb's attitude.

"What's wrong with you?" she asked Adam's older, usually wiser, brother. "Are you this insecure with your position within the service that you have to begrudge your very own brother this amazing opportunity? Adam's a great marshal, and he deserves his spot on what's apparently an intriguing case. I'm sorry, Caleb, but right now, your behavior strikes me as being childish and petty."

Caleb pushed himself up from his seat and laughed. On his way out of the room, he tipped his bottle of beer at Adam. "Childish and petty. Yup. That's me."

Thankfully, Adam's dad and Allie's mom were seated three rows ahead and had missed the whole awkward exchange, as had Joe's former in-laws.

"What's gotten into him?" Charity asked once Caleb had left the room.

"Beats me," Adam said, downing a swig of his beer.

"Under any other circumstance, I'd tell you to go have it out with him. He shouldn't be treating you like that. But tonight, I want you all to myself."

Kissing her again, he said, "I couldn't agree more."

AFTER MAKING LOVE twice to his wife-to-be in a swanky Parisian-themed suite Gillian had decorated just for them, Adam should've been tired, but the second his eyes closed, his brain sprung wide awake.

He could throttle Caleb for the way he'd acted around Charity. What the hell had he been thinking? Popping off like that. Charity finding out about his suspension wasn't going to help anything. In fact, in just the couple weeks since he'd placed himself in intensive therapy, Adam felt as if he'd made great strides in overcoming the demons that'd been like acid to his soul ever since Angela's death.

Sure, probably the right thing to do in this case would be to tell Charity the whole truth about what his secret mission was, but this was one of those times where maybe there wasn't any definitive right or wrong. Just gray.

The only person who could ultimately judge if he was doing right was Charity, but he couldn't take the risk in telling her. Not now, with the wedding so close. If he told her, and she didn't understand—didn't understand to the point that she didn't even want to marry him—what then? How would he survive without her?

With her, and the baby who was on the way, his life would once again be in sync. Everything would make sense again. After slipping his ring on Charity's finger, all wrongs would magically be right.

While they were on their way to Paris, he'd tell her everything, but until then, he couldn't take the risk.

"OH, SWEETIE," Charity gushed into the Parisian suite's phone to Adam the Thursday afternoon before their Saturday wedding. She'd accrued so much vacation time over the years that she'd taken off the week before the big event and three weeks after. Even though they'd be in France only two weeks, she figured there would be plenty to do once they got home, what with moving Adam out of his apartment and into her condo, where they'd decided to live. "You're not going to believe the setting Gillian and her team of magicians have made for our big event. The solarium was already gorgeous, but we'll be taking our vows on the prettiest altar/bridge thingee Gillian had built over the deep end of the pool, right by the waterfall. At first, I was afraid the water might be too loud for our friends and family to hear us make our vows, but Gillian's gardener assured me he can lessen the flow, so that it's not a roar, but more of a happy trickle."

Adam laughed, and Charity's heart swelled. "Sounds perfect, angel. I can't wait to see it."

"You'll be here tomorrow night, right? We have the rehearsal dinner and Gracie's fixing—"

"Relax. I'll be there. After work, I just need to go by my apartment and pack a few things."

"Want me to do it for you in the morning? Gillian's got so many crews handling most everything, I'm usually dead weight around here."

"No," Adam said sharply. "I can handle it."

"Really," she said, glad the phone was cordless so she could flop into a more comfortable position on the bed. "I don't mind. It'd give me something to do. I'm getting nervous—no, not really nervous, just excited, you know. It seems like I've been waiting forever for this day to come and now that it's almost here, I don't quite know what to do with myself." She sighed, fingering her hair. "All this nervous energy. It's balling up inside. Too bad you're not here," she said with a sexy purr. "I'm sure we could figure some creative way to eliminate excess energy."

"Hold tight," he said with a chuckle. "I'll be there to assist you in twenty minutes."

"I wish," she said, joining in on his laughter. "Luckily, it won't be too long now till I never have to be without you again."

"You got that right. So," he said, "you're going to stay at Gillian's in the morning, right? Do the whole blushing bride thing while I run by and get my clothes?"

"If that's what you want, but I don't see why I can't save you some time by—"

"It's what I want," he said.

"All right."

Caw! Caw!

"What was that?" he asked.

"Gillian was afraid the solarium birds might have an *accident* on the tables or a guest, so she temporarily caged them, and all of us now have the pleasure of big, noisy birds in our rooms."

He laughed. "On second thought, with that racket going on all night, maybe I'm glad I'm not there."

Caw! Caw! Caw!

"Yeah, but just think," Charity said. "All that noise would make a pretty good dampener for certain other noises…" She made a kissy sound into the phone.

"Stop. You're killing me," he said. "Maybe I could make it in fifteen minutes if I ran every light and stop sign?"

"Don't you dare. The last thing we need is Franks firing you for bailing on your post. You just finish up your portion of this job, and I'll be here, on one of my last nights as a single girl, sharing the bed with the hottest guy in the house."

"And who would that be?" Adam asked.

Grinning, casting an indulgent look at the handsome fella draped across the foot of the bed, she said, "That would be Barney."

Laughing, Adam said, "See you tomorrow, Almost-Mrs. Logue. I love you."

"Love you, too," she said into the dead phone. Hands trembling, Charity returned the handset to its charging pad.

Why, when she should've been deliriously happy, did she suddenly have this feeling of dread?

Was Caleb still giving Adam trouble?

There was only one way to find out.

Caw! Caw!

She hopped up from the bed, gave Barney a pat, the obnoxious bird a glare, then snatched her keys and purse from a table near the suite's double doors. She'd nearly made it to the mansion's front door when Gillian rounded a corner, asking, "Where do you think you're going? You have a dress fitting in ten minutes."

"I can't," Charity said, darting around the woman who would soon be her sister-in-law, but who'd already become a dear friend.

"Honey, what's wrong?" Gillian grasped Charity's upper arm. "Did you and Adam have a fight? You did just get off the phone with him, right?"

"Yes, we were on the phone. But, no, everything's great between us. It's Caleb I have a problem with. I'm going in to Portland now. To the office. It's high time I had it out with that pigheaded, selfish, egotistical—"

"Whoa," Gillian said, pulling Charity into a hug. "You're shaking. "Come here—" she pulled her onto a nearby chair "—all this excitement can't be good for the baby."

"The baby's fine. It's Caleb you should be worried about. When I get my hands on him, he's going to—"

"Seriously," Gillian said. "Calm down and give

my big brother the benefit of the doubt. With you and Adam out of the office, he's been under a lot of pressure to pick up the slack. I'm sure work stress is what must've caused whatever he said—not anything Adam might've done."

"Gillian?" Charity looked up, not liking the stricken look on her friend's face. "I never said Caleb and I had words."

"I—I didn't say you did," Gillian said, glancing away. "I just assumed that must be why you're upset with him. Believe me," she said with a short laugh, "if anyone understands how aggravating Caleb can be, it's me. And my best advice," she said, dropping into the chair beside Charity's, putting her hand on her knee, "is to just ignore him. No denying the man can be a pain, but he loves Adam—and you."

"Then why is he giving Adam such grief?"

"What exactly has Adam told you?"

"Nothing," Charity said. "That's the problem. She relayed the words exchanged between the brothers over Thanksgiving. "Don't you think that sounds odd?"

"It's a guy thing," Gillian said, tsking off Charity's concerns. "No matter how much you love them, they're ultimately a mystery. All we can do is stand by and hope they don't hurt themselves."

"Hurt themselves?" Charity leaned forward. "You mean, like they're at such odds they might fight?"

"No, no," Gillian said. "Don't pay any attention to me. I meant that more in the cosmic sense. You know, how guys are always doing some boneheaded thing we have to rescue them from."

"Then does that mean Adam or Caleb are in some kind of trouble?"

"Not at all." She glanced at her watch. "Whoa, we've been out here chatting for so long you've almost missed your appointment. The tailor should be all set up in the front parlor."

Charity glanced toward the door. "Then you don't think I should have a talk with Caleb? Clear the air before the rehearsal dinner?"

"You could go," Gillian said. "But ultimately, it'd probably be a waste of time. Now, if you miss this last fitting, on the other hand, you'll really be wasting time because we'll have to find you a whole new gown by Saturday."

"All right," Charity said, the lingering suspicion that not all was right still in her gut. "I'll let it go. But if Caleb so much as looks at me or Adam cross-eyed, he's going to get it."

THE SECOND Charity was busy with the tailor, Gillian high-tailed it to Joe's office and shut the door. "When I get my hands on that brother of mine, I'm going to strangle him."

"Which one?" Joe asked, hanging up his phone.

"Actually, all three."

"Charity wise up and figure out Adam isn't on some mysterious mission, but hiding at his apartment?"

"No, but I'm afraid she's close. Oh, Joe," she said, flopping into the guest chair in front of his desk. "I'm so mad at Adam for keeping his suspension from her. If he'd just fessed up at the time about how he'd left his post to be with her, I think she'd have understood, but now…" She shook her head. "And Caleb—what's he thinking to have even gotten himself involved? And seeing how he's up to his neck in this, he should've just kept his big mouth shut."

"What'd he do?"

"Nothing concrete. Just enough to give our bride reason to be suspicious. I swear, Joe, if that brother of mine does something to foul up this wedding…"

"Relax," Joe said, leaving his desk to rub her shoulders. "These past weeks, I've spent a lot of time talking with Adam. I think he's finally got his head on straight."

"I know," she said. "It's not Adam I'm currently upset with, it's Caleb."

"Women," Joe said, rolling his eyes.

"Men," Gillian said, shaking her head.

"You know you love us." Joe knelt beside her, stealing a kiss.

"Okay, I love *you*," she said. "But not my crazy brothers."

Barney thumped his tail against Joe's desk.

"Sorry, Barn." She reached down to give his ear a rub. "I love you, too."

THOUGH, as far as Adam was concerned, Caleb was an informational bomb waiting to blow, much to his pleasant surprise, his big brother seemed back to his old charming self during the rehearsal dinner—at least when the whole gang was gathered.

The few times they'd been on their own, he hadn't bothered disguising grouchy stares.

Now, thankfully, Adam was on the crowded dance floor with his beautiful bride-to-be. Usually this space, located on the far side of the indoor river that ultimately twisted its way to the waterfall, was the kids' minigolf course. But for this special occasion, Gillian must've paid a fortune to have it covered in wood parquet. Surrounded by tall and stubby palms along with sweet-smelling flowering shrubs, despite the slow Christmas ballad the band was playing, Adam would've sworn he was in Tahiti instead of Oregon.

"Hasn't this been fun?" Charity said, resting her cheek against his chest.

"Yeah. Gillian and Gracie sure know how to throw a party."

"Don't forget me," Allie said, grinning beside them, apparently content dancing in her husband's arms. "I showed the party supply guys where to park."

"I could never forget you," Charity said, leaving Adam to pull her bridesmaid into a hug. "Thanks for all you've done."

"Hey," Adam complained. "What's the deal? Stealing my girl?"

"Here she is," Allie teased, delivering Charity into Adam's outstretched arms. "Back all safe and sound."

"I never worried she wouldn't be safe," Adam said. "I just missed her."

Caleb snorted.

"You got something to say?" Adam asked.

Caleb just shot him a look, taking Allie by her hand to lead her off the crowded floor.

"What was that about?" Charity asked.

"Nothing. Just my brother's sick sense of humor."

"Funny," she said. "But I don't find him amusing."

"Forget him," he urged. "Focus on us. Just think, tomorrow at this time, you'll be my wife."

"Mmm…" she said, easing back into his arms. "I can't wait."

"Me, neither," Adam said, glad Bug's back was to the powwow Caleb and Beau and their wives were having over by the champagne fountain. Odds were, they were discussing him, but by this time tomorrow, once Charity was his wife, what they said wouldn't matter. Because she'd have vowed to love him forever. And at that point, there'd be no need for them to ever keep secrets from each other again.

"YOU LOOK BEAUTIFUL," Steph said, adjusting Charity's veil. Gillian had transformed the ultrafeminine garden room off the solarium into a dressing room fit for royalty. Though it was Christmas, it felt more like July, with warm sun streaming through a wall of paned windows and fragrant orchids and roses filling every spare corner. Happy love songs had been playing steadily for an hour, only increasing Charity's sense of giddy excitement.

"Thank you," Charity said, stepping back from the cheval mirror she'd been gazing into to pull her sister into a hug. "I feel beautiful. Beyond belief blessed. For the longest time, I was afraid this day wouldn't come, but now—"

"Is it time?" Steph asked.

"For what? Heading down the aisle? I thought we were ahead of schedule? I need your help handing out my bridesmaid gifts. I found the most darling Swarovski crystal ladybugs that—"

"Calm down," Steph said, applying more face powder, then blush. "I was asking if it's time for me to tell you I told you so."

"About what?" Charity asked.

"Oh, remember a couple months back when a certain someone moped around, worrying that just because she was one of the guys, she might never land one?"

"I never said that," Charity complained, trying to hide her easy grin. "I'm a hardened marshal. I don't even have time for boys."

"Uh-huh." Steph winked. "Lie all you want. I just want it said I was right."

"What were you right about?" their mom asked.
Steph relayed the story.

"Yes," their mother said. "In this case, I have to agree with Stephanie. In the past, Charity, you have been known to borrow worries when you couldn't find enough of your own."

"What's that supposed to mean?" Charity asked.

"Nothing," her mother said, fussing even more over the veil Steph had already adjusted at least ten times. "Just that in all the years you've feared never having a family of your own, your sister, dad and I have loved you enough to know someday, some very wise man would snap you up."

"Aw…" Charity blinked back tears.

"Don't you cry!" Gillian bustled over. "You'll muss your makeup."

"I'm fine," Charity said. "Sort of." Fanning her face, she smiled through happy tears. The only way this day could be brighter was if her twin brother had lived to share it with her. It was her fervent hope that while Craig couldn't be here in person, he was at least here in spirit. "Oh, who am I kidding? I'm a wreck. But a happy one. And speaking of wrecks, has anyone seen my future hubby?"

"I saw Uncle Adam," Meggie said, looking beyond adorable in the white co-flower girl dress that was a pint-size miniature of Charity's. Barney wandered up behind her, a ring pillow strapped to his collar.

He sat on his hind legs, trying to have a good

scratch at it with his right front paw, but Meggie took her duties very seriously and pushed his paw away.

Chrissy, also a flower girl, wearing an even smaller version of Charity's dress, said, "Bad dog, Barney."

"What was he doing?" Charity asked the next-to-the-youngest of her bridal party.

"Barney was trying to knock over his pillow, but I stopped him." Meggie proudly beamed at her ingenuity.

All assembled laughed.

"I know what Barney was doing, sweetie," Charity said. "I was talking about your uncle Adam. What was he doing?"

"Oh," Meggie said with a wide smile. "He was playing video games. He was beating Daddy really bad, but Daddy said that was just because he'd had so much time to practice."

"Meggie…" Gillian switched to fussing with Meggie's hair bow. "How about peeking out the dressing room door to see if Aunt Charity's daddy is ready."

"But, Mommy," Meggie said, "I was talking about Uncle Adam. Ever since he doesn't work anymore, he's like the best ever at video games. He's always beating Daddy really bad, and it's funny when Daddy pretends to cry."

Charity knelt beside the little girl. "What did you mean," she asked, "about Uncle Adam not working?"

"You know," the little girl said, tugging a flyaway

curl, ultimately putting it in her mouth. "About how Uncle Adam's been hiding at his apartment. Me and Daddy went to see him lots of times, and boy," she said, eyes wide, "was it ever messy. If Mommy had been there, she'd give him a time-out."

"Meggie," Gillian said, "that's enough."

"Did she just say what I thought she did?" Charity quietly asked, a part of her not wanting to know.

"No," Allie said, hustling over to further fiddle with the bride's veil.

Charity brushed her away. "Would everyone please leave my veil alone and tell me the truth? I knew all along something was funky about what Adam's been doing, but—"

A knock sounded on the door, then the wedding planner poked her head through. "Places, everyone. We're ready to begin."

"Wait," Charity said. "I have to—"

"What you have to do—" the brassy woman Charity had never particularly liked, gave her a gentle shove toward the door "—is get down that aisle. Everyone's waiting for you."

As if on autopilot, though her head was reeling and a strange hum had started in her ears, Charity allowed herself to be shuffled along, absorbed into the big event's carefully choreographed flow. But even as the seconds ticked by, carrying her ever closer to the man she truly felt was her soul mate, doubts crept in.

What if what Meggie had said was true? That Adam really hadn't been working? Then what had he been doing? Why would he lie to her? What possible motivation could he have had? Other than hiding something he'd done that he'd known she wouldn't be pleased about.

"Gillian!" Charity said in a stage whisper, yanking her out of the bridesmaid's line-up. Meggie and Chrissy were already grinning their way down the aisle. Barney had even stopped trying to scratch his ring pillow.

Friends and family twisted in their seats. Everyone she knew and loved was here, straining for a glimpse at her and the dress that must've cost Gillian more than a small country's yearly budget. All of these people she loved had come to see a wedding. After their vows, Charity could drill Adam for the next fifty years. Now, the smart choice—the only choice—was to walk down that aisle…right?

"Charity," Gillian said. "Get the stricken look off your face. Let it rest. Whatever Adam did or didn't do doesn't matter now. It's your wedding day. Smile."

"It matters if he lied to me," Charity said, her voice oddly disconnected from the rest of her body. Hot and dizzy, part of her felt as if she were floating. As if some other poor bride had heard this devastating news. "Tell me the truth. Has Adam been on a case all these weeks, or was he suspended from work?"

"All right," Gillian said, glancing down the aisle

at her panicked-looking brother. "Here it is. That day you got shot? Adam walked out of the courthouse in order to see you."

"But he had Caleb's permission."

"No, honey," Gillian said, hand on her satin, lace and-pearl-covered arm. "He walked out against explicit orders to continue manning his security post. For all that team knew, the shooter could've come after the judge at any moment, but Adam chose to leave the judge and go to you."

Charity wasn't sure how to process this news. In front of her, beyond all those smiling faces of friends and family, at the faraway end of the long, orchid-and-fern-lined aisle, stood Adam, so tall and handsome and…

Queasy-looking?

He flashed her a cheesy grin. The one he used when trying to get himself out of the doghouse.

Right at this very second, Adam knew what Gillian was telling her. He knew, and he was afraid. After going off on her that night in the motel about not telling him the whole truth about Cookie's rock incident, he'd flat-out lied about something as serious as his having been suspended from the marshal's service.

Though Allie and Gracie had already made it to the business end of the long aisle, Gillian and Steph still remained.

"Ladies," the wedding planner hissed, wildly gesturing to the last bridesmaid and maid of honor. "Poste haste, if you please."

"Charity?" Gillian asked. "You okay? If Adam didn't love you so much, he never would've—"

With her pulse pounding in her ears, Charity looked to her sister, father, to all the guests gazing at her with concern. She'd been blessed to have not been cursed with much morning sickness, but now, sour bile rose in her throat. Placing her five pounds worth of white orchids and roses with the crystal ladybug poking out the top on a nearby side table, she took a deep breath. Stilled her hands by resting them on her churning stomach.

If Adam would flat-out lie about something as big as this, what else would he lie about? Had he already lied about? Was he just as much in love with Angela as ever, only now that Charity carried his child, family pressure was making him go through with this wedding?

Suddenly her glamorous dress was weighing her down, reminding her who she was. A homely female marshal whose idea of a good time was sitting around cataloging bugs while dressed in ratty old sweats.

She'd tried elevating herself to a new standard. To a place where, if she was lucky, a man like Adam would love her. Funny, though, how now that he supposedly loved her, she had serious doubts. All those times he'd said he wasn't good enough for her? She should've listened. She should've run as fast as her legs would carry her.

She should've done all that months earlier, but instead, with one last heartbreaking look down the aisle at the man she thought she'd be spending the rest of her life with, Charity made up for past mistakes with a few brave current moves.

She told her father, Steph and Gillian sorry and that she loved them.

Hiked up her miles of satin train.

Then ran for the door and one of the many limos she prayed would still be outside.

Chapter Sixteen

"Bug, wait!" Adam cried, knowing the instant he'd seen the cloud descend over his Bug's beautiful face that his sister had told her the truth. After charging down the aisle, not giving a damn what people thought, he asked his sister, "What's the matter with you? Why'd you have to tell her? You've ruined everything."

"*I've* ruined everything?" Her laugh was brittle. "Trust me, Adam, you botched this one all on your on. I was backpedaling for you as fast as I could, but tell me, how was I supposed to smooth over the fact that for all these weeks leading up to your wedding, you've been lying like a dirty rug?"

The crowd of more than two hundred began to chatter, their condemning tones hitting Adam like a killer wave, roaring in his ears.

The sweet scent of too many flowers crushed him. Closed in on him, making him nauseous as hell.

Worst part of all of this was that Gillian was right. Every ounce of pain he was feeling was his own damned fault. He was a fool for trying to keep the truth from Charity.

He was an even bigger fool for believing screwups like him got second chances at a happy ending.

"Well?" Gillian asked. "Aren't you going to go after her?"

"Won't do much good." With his hands stuffed into his tux pockets, Adam slowly exhaled. "She hates me. What could I ever say to make her give me another chance? She's already given me about two dozen."

"And so just like that," Joe said, stepping behind his wife, slipping his arms around her waist, resting his chin on her shoulder, "you're going to give up?"

"Couldn't have asked that better myself," Dr. Margaret said, parking herself beside Gillian and Joe.

Thank God, Charity's dad and sister were off talking to her mom. Adam's immediate surroundings were crowded enough without throwing beadyeyed in-laws into the mix.

"Look," Adam said. "I screwed up. Again. I don't even want her to take me back. Lord knows I don't deserve her."

"No," Dr. Margaret said. "You don't deserve her, but you need her. And though I haven't yet had the privilege of meeting your *Bug,* I have a sneaking suspicion she also needs you."

"All that's well and good," Adam said, "but how am I supposed to convince her of this supposed need? All she really wanted was a baby. Now that she's got that, what does she need me for? The woman ran out on our wedding. I'm taking that as a pretty clear sign she despises me."

"She might think she does at the moment, but how about giving her a heartfelt apology and one of those cute grins of yours?"

"I have a cute grin?" he asked, eyebrows raised.

"If you didn't," Dr. Margaret said, pulling him into a hug, "then why would I have put up with you all this time?"

"Excellent point," Gillian said. "Now, Adam, go after her already. I've got more than two hundred guests to keep entertained until you bring back the bride, and believe me, after one or two minutes of Joe's singing, they're not going to be happy."

"Hey," Joe complained. "I'm a fantastic singer."

Gillian snorted. "When you're in the shower, but—"

"While you two hash all this out," Adam said, "I'm going to go find my future wife."

Adam was just about to the mansion's front door when Sam came running up behind him. "Hey, Logue! Wait up!"

"This isn't the best time," Adam said with a sigh.

"It's the only time," Sam said, raising his chin. "I just have to say for the record that if Charity doesn't forgive you, I get dibs."

"Dibs?" With clenched fists, Adam said, "She's carrying *my* child."

"I don't mind. I'll love him or her all the same."

Bam.

Adam landed his best right to the jerk-off's cocky, self-assured face.

Then, while Sam stood there rubbing his already reddening jaw, Adam said, "Charity's *mine*. Her baby's mine. I love her. And if it takes me every day for the rest of my life to get her back, then I guess I'd best get started."

Grinning as Adam stormed out the door, Sam said, "Thanks. That's all I needed to know."

AFTER AN HOUR limo ride back to her condo, then thirty more minutes tracking down the building super because she'd left her key and purse at Gillian and Joe's, Charity was finally right where she wanted to be. Wearing her rattiest sweats and T-shirt, sitting cross-legged on the sofa with football on TV and a gorgeous, Central African *Dicronorrhina derbyana* in front of her that she'd received by mail nearly four weeks earlier, but because of all the planning she'd been doing for her stupid wedding to that stupid man she now never wanted to see again, she hadn't yet had time to mount.

Fortunately, now that Adam was out of her life, she'd have all the time in the world for bug collecting and watching sports and…

Who was she trying to kid?

Hot, racking tears started with no signs of let-

ting up. And then she got sick. And then she remembered she was carrying Adam's baby, and that
no matter how hard she wished him out of her life,
she knew darned well she'd always love the guy.
She just couldn't ever trust him enough to marry
him. Which—

Her thoughts were interrupted by banging on her
condo's door.

"Charity!" Adam hollered loud enough to rouse
crotchety old Mrs. Kleypus down the hall. Sure
enough, Gringo had already started his shrill
barking. "I know you're in there. The limo dispatch
record shows this is where the driver dropped you
off. Open up!"

Great. Just fan-freakin'-tastic. Why had she fall-
en in love with a guy who found missing people for
a living?

"Sweetheart," he said, sounding suspiciously
short, as if he'd knelt in front of the door and was
talking through the eighth-inch slat between the
carpet and bottom of the door. "I know I messed up.
Big-time. I'm a liar and creep and scum and lower
than any life form presently on the planet."

True.

Nibbling her lower lip, trying not to burst into
tears again more because she didn't want to make
herself sick than because of lingering feelings she
might have for—

"Angel, I love you. If it makes a difference, I've

spent these last weeks trying to make myself better—
for you. When I got suspended, I was ashamed. Not
because I left my post to go to you—I'd do that again
in a heartbeat. But because I love you so much, I want
to be everything for you. A great marshal. Someone
you can be proud of. I want to be a great husband and
dad and friend and—"

"Would you shut up down there!" Mrs. Kleypus
shouted from two doors down the hall. "You sound
like a bleating cat! She's obviously not in there! Even
if she were, I'd tell her to—"

Charity unlocked the door. "Mind your own business!" she shouted down the hall. "My fiancé was
right in the middle of a good speech."

The old woman harrumphed before slamming her
door.

Gringo kept right on barking.

"Get in here," Charity said to Adam, dragging him
inside. First she kissed him hard on the lips, then
slugged him equally as hard in his gut.

"Ouch," he complained, rubbing his abs. "What
was that for?"

"You even have to ask?"

Grimacing, he said, "Guess I had it coming."

"And then some. Dammit, Logue, I trusted you.
Do you have any idea how many nights I sat here
worrying because I thought you might be off, getting
yourself shot?"

"I'm sorry."

"Sorry's not good enough!" she roared in frustration. "I don't even know what I want from you. I can't imagine what you could do to make up for this big a lie. We're supposed to be a team. Best friends. Partners. What? Am I not worthy of the truth? Am I—"

"You're perfection," he said. "That's why I lied. Because I was scared of losing you—not to a bullet, but due to my own stupidity. I was afraid that if I'd told you I'd been suspended, you'd see it as the last straw and want nothing more to do with me."

"And so that's why Caleb's been so cagey? Not because he's been jealous, but resenting his role in helping you keep this from me?"

"Yeah."

"Why did he? Hell, for that matter, why'd the whole office keep this from me?"

"Because like me, they *all* love you. And who wouldn't? You're sweet and funny and sexy and smart and a good shot, and if you agree to forgive me, I'll even promise to change every poopy diaper for every kid we're ever blessed to have."

"Quit trying to butter me up," Charity said, wiping still more tears. "Although if I decide to take you back, I'll hold you to that poopy diaper promise."

"Sure. Whatever."

"And even though a promise like that'll go a long way toward redeeming your many sins, I'm still mad at you."

"Can't say as I blame you." He pulled her into his

arms. "But how long are you going to stay mad? Because back at Gillian and Joe's we've got an awful lot of folks sitting around, waiting to see us get married."

"There's a problem with that," she said.

"What?"

"I honestly don't know that we should get married. I mean, you said you wouldn't lie to me again, and I appreciate the fact that you used this time alone to get your head in a better place, but—"

Sweeping her into his arms, he carried her to the bedroom, landing her on the bed. "Stay here."

"But—"

"Where's the phone?" he asked, eyeing the empty charging pad.

"I must've left it in the living room. Why? Who do you need to call?"

"I was going to call my sister to tell her that after I thoroughly make love to you, then give you your wedding present, that—"

"You got me a present?" she asked, sitting up in the bed. "Can I have it now? It might help me make up my mind over whether or not to marry you." She winked.

He groaned. "Be right back. It's in the coat closet."

Charity knew she was taking a risk in trusting again, but so was Adam. Bottom line, try all she might to convince herself she didn't love him, she did. Messed up heart and all.

Who knew? Maybe in their case, the *for worse*

part of their vows had come first. And from here on out, there'd be nothing but *for better* between them.

"Here you go," he said, presenting her with a tin-foil-wrapped box. For a bow, he'd taped a Twinkies to the top.

"Great wrapping," she said, not sure whether to eat the decoration first or to commence with opening.

"Thanks. Took me an hour to get all the foil nice and flat."

"I'll bet," she said, working hard at hiding a grin.

If her mind hadn't been made up before about taking him back, the sight of what was in the box would've had her back in her wedding dress and down the aisle in five seconds flat.

"Oh, Adam," she said, eyes tearing this time because any man who could make her something as goofy-wonderful as this would definitely be worth holding on to for the long haul. "It's amazing."

Careful not to knock any heads off, she withdrew a mini-clay replica of her car, behind the wheel of which sat a handmade clay beetle body with a human head—hers. In the passenger seat, was beetle-Adam. In the back sat three baby beetles with cherubic cheeks and antennae.

While she stared in wonder at the detail that must've taken him days to complete, he said, "I love you."

She gingerly set the car on the nightstand, then leaned into his waiting arms. "I love you, too. It's an amazing gift. Thank you."

He shrugged. "I was going to get you that Indonesian *Euchirus longimanus* you've been wanting, but somehow that seemed more appropriate for your birthday. Anyway, thank you, too."

"For what? Your gift is back in our suite—and it's just a watch. Nowhere near as much fun as this."

"Don't you get it?" he asked.

"What?"

"You and the baby are my gift. I adore you." And he proceeded to show her just how much for the next hour.

"JOE?" Gillian glared at her watch. "Where do you suppose they are? Are they even together? Has my brother driven off a cliff? Or did he find Charity and she shot him? Which, I can't in all honesty say I'd blame her for."

"Calm down," Joe said, snatching a kiss. "They'll get here when they get here."

And eventually, they did. And the wedding was spectacular—better than even Gillian had ever dared hope for. Partially because her dear mother was finally getting at least one of her children to be married in a Christmas wedding, but mostly because now that Adam was finally married off, everyone in her family was wholly and completely in love.

Well—everyone might be in love, but not everyone was official. But seeing how her father planned to pop the question to Allie's mom while they were in Paris, and how Gillian had long since gotten the

framework in place should the need arise for a New
Year's Paris wedding, to say the entire family wasn't
married was at this point a mere technicality!

Unless she counted the kids…

"Joe?" she asked.

"Uh-huh?"

"How long in advance do you think I'll have to
make reservations for Meggie to be married somewhere off-the-charts exotic?"

"Like Fiji?"

"No. I was thinking *big*. More like the Taj Mahal."

Epilogue

Two years later

"You finally did it," Adam said, shaking Caleb's hand. They stood in Gillian and Joe's solarium, talking over a jazz band squawking louder than the damn tropical birds Gillian had forgotten to cage. But then seeing how his sister was due any day with her and Joe's third child, he guessed she was entitled to be a little *off* in her usual party-planning finesse. "Now that Franks finally retired, you're Oregon's youngest presidentially appointed U.S. Marshal. How's it feel?"

"Great," Caleb said. "But not half as good as seeing you hold this little new one. Congratulations, man. I had my doubts about you ever getting your head out of your—well…" He smoothed the newborn girl's blond curls. "Out of your *you know* long enough for you to realize what a great thing you and Charity share. But now that you have, I couldn't be happier."

"Thanks," Adam said. "I think."

Charity bustled up. To Caleb, she said, "Now that you're boss, does this mean we get extra vacation?"

Caleb snorted. "Not hardly. If anything, because you're a Logue, you get less. Want to be in the center of a nepotism scandal?"

Allie joined their circle. "I know Gillian and Joe are hosting this big reception to honor your new position, but do you think just once you could lose that furrow between your eyebrows and relax enough to enjoy the fruits of your labor?"

"Maybe," Caleb said, wrapping his arm around his wife's waist. "Given the right incentive." He whispered something in Allie's ear.

She giggled, then said to all of them, "What do you know? He came up with just the right thing."

After Caleb and Allie snuck off to no doubt their favorite Wild West suite, Charity asked Adam, "Want to trade babies?"

Eyebrows raised, he said, "Don't tell me, Duncan went again?"

"Meggie and Chrissy gave him a few too many of those fancy puffy cheese things."

"Aw, man," Adam complained. "You know how after he eats rich foods his diapers smell."

"Yep," she said, holding out their son to him. "Which is why I save all of his most special diapers for you. After all—" she winked "—a promise is a promise."

Watching his gorgeous wife and baby girl flit off

for a dance with Bear, Adam figured he was just about the happiest guy alive. Poopy diapers or not, when his Bug agreed to marry him, he'd by far gotten the better end of the deal.

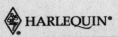

HARLEQUIN®

American ROMANCE®

IS PROUD TO PRESENT A GUEST APPEARANCE BY

QUILL
BOOK
AWARD
WINNING
AUTHOR

NEW YORK TIMES bestselling author

DEBBIE MACOMBER

The Wyoming Kid

The story of an ex–rodeo cowboy,
a schoolteacher and their journey to the altar.

"Best-selling Macomber, with more than
100 romances and women's fiction titles
to her credit, sure has a way of pleasing readers."
—*Booklist* on *Between Friends*

**The Wyoming Kid is available from
Harlequin American Romance in July 2006.**

BRINGS YOU THE LATEST IN
Vicki Hinze's
WAR GAMES
MINISERIES

Double Dare

December 2005

A plot to release the deadly DR-27 supervirus at a crowded mall? Not U.S. Air Force captain Maggie Holt's idea of Christmas cheer. Forget the mistletoe— Maggie, with the help of scientist Justin Crowe, has to stop a psycho terrorist before she can even think of enjoying Christmas kisses.

Available at your favorite retail outlet.

Silhouette® Desire®

Page-turning drama…

Exotic, glamorous locations…

Intense emotion and passionate seduction…

Sheikhs, princes and billionaire tycoons…

This summer, may we suggest:

THE SHEIKH'S DISOBEDIENT BRIDE
by Jane Porter

On sale June.

AT THE GREEK TYCOON'S BIDDING
by Cathy Williams

On sale July.

THE ITALIAN MILLIONAIRE'S VIRGIN WIFE

On sale August.

With new titles to choose from every month,
discover a world of romance in our books written
by internationally bestselling authors.

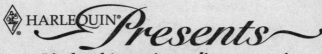

HARLEQUIN® *Presents*

It's the ultimate in quality romance!

Available wherever Harlequin books are sold.

www.eHarlequin.com

HPGEN06